Goat Boy

Chronicles

Goat Boy Chronicles

THE BIG PIG STAMPEDE

written by **BOB HARTMAN**

illustrated by Amerigo Pinelli

THE BIG PIG
STAMPEDE

Tyndale House Publishers, Inc.
Carol Stream, Illinois

Visit Tyndale online at www.tyndale.com.

TYNDALE and Tyndale's quill logo are registered trademarks of Tyndale House Publishers, Inc.

The Big Pig Stampede

Copyright © 2015 by Bob Hartman. All rights reserved.

Illustrations copyright © Amerigo Pinelli. All rights reserved.

Designed by Jacqueline L. Nuñez

Edited by Caleb Sjogren

Published in association with the literary agency of William K. Jensen Literary Agency, 119 Bampton Court, Eugene, OR 97404.

The Big Pig Stampede is a work of fiction. Where real people, events, establishments, organizations, or locales appear, they are used fictiously. All other elements of the novel are drawn from the author's imagination.

For manufacturing information regarding this product, please call 1-800-323-9400.

ISBN 978-1-4964-0865-5

Printed in the United States of America

21	20	19	18	17	16	15
7	6	5	4	3	2	1

For Malachi

Contents

Chapter One

WHERE ME AND BUG MAKE A DEAL. SORT OF.

My brother was the first one to call me Goat Boy.

I'm eleven. He's thirteen. He thinks he knows everything. And he's sort of a bit of a jerk.

No. That's not exactly true. There's no "sort of" or "bit of" about it. He's a jerk.

All right, I did have a goat I took care of. I mean, I still do. That's one of my jobs. So what?

"Everybody has to pitch in." That's what my dad always says. So he runs the market stall. And my brother helps him buy the stuff we sell. And I take care of whatever animals we pick up along the way.

I like animals. I'm good at taking care of them. What's the big deal?

It's not like I call *him* names.

"Hello, Cheap Trinket Boy!"

"Yo, Mr. Busted Pottery!"

Okay, he'd probably punch me if I did. (And he punches really hard.) But I don't do it. That's the point.

Anyway, Goat Boy stuck. Mostly because he just kept saying it and wouldn't shut up about it.

And that's why my friend Bug shouted, "Hey, Goat Boy!" when he ran up to the stall tonight, and not "Hey, Gideon!" which is my real name, which he knows.

To be fair, I do call him Bug. But I don't actually know his real name, because he likes Bug and refuses to go by anything else. Or tell anybody else what his real name actually is. So I'm sort of stuck.

And yeah, he's called Bug partly because he's small. But also because he can be kind of annoying. Oh, and because one time he ate a melon that had bugs all over it. Which he went ahead and ate too.

Honest, I nearly vomit every time I think about it. But it didn't bother Bug at all.

So Bug shouted, "Hey, Goat Boy!" and I shouted back, "Hey, Bug!" and that's when he asked me, "Has your dad got any wine for sale?"

"Yeah," I said. "He's got some wine. How much do you need?"

"As much as you have. There's this big wedding on the other side of town, and they ran out.

So the word on the street is they'll buy whatever anyone's got."

Bug's dad runs a stall like ours. We all sort of travel around together, from town to town. My dad says Bug's dad is the best market trader he ever met. And that's saying something, because lots of people say that about *my* dad. So if there was a deal going, and Bug's dad was part of it, I knew my dad would want to get in on it as well.

Bug and I ran to the stall to tell him, but the only person there was my big brother.

"Sam!" I shouted. (Short for Samson. Known for punching people. Of course.) "Where's Dad?"

He looked down at me. He always looks down at me. "Who wants to know?"

"I want to know! Who do you think?" I shouted.

"He's off somewhere, doing a deal," Sam said. "You'll just have to wait."

"There isn't time to wait," Bug whispered in his insisting, bugging sort of way. "They need the wine *now!*"

I figured that. But I also figured if I told my brother, he'd sell the wine and take all the credit for it, and I'd still just be Goat Boy. This was my

chance to prove that I could be a
brilliant market trader too.

So I grabbed two
skins full of wine, chucked
another at Bug, and
said, "Run!"

"What do you two think you're
doing?" my brother shouted as we disappeared
down an alley. I knew he wouldn't come after us.
He needed to stay and watch the stall. And I knew

my dad wouldn't mind, either. Not if I came back with a pile of coins.

Bug led the way, through a maze of back streets. We went as quickly as we could, but the wine skins were full and felt heavier the farther we ran.

Finally we arrived at a big house, with torches blazing and people dancing and servants buzzing in and out. Bug grabbed a boy about our age and we put our wineskins on a table to show him. The boy's name was Shem. He was tall and scrawny and had a front tooth missing. He was one of the servants, and also Bug's contact.

"Where do you want us to put the wine?" Bug asked. "And where do we get paid?" Bug's dad had taught him well. *Paid* is always the most important word.

Shem looked kind of embarrassed. "Umm . . . well . . . we don't really need the wine anymore," he muttered.

"What do you mean?" Bug bugged. "You ran out. You've got a huge crowd here. There's no way you already found enough wine for everybody in this place."

Shem shrugged. "That's what we thought. But then this woman came up to us." He pointed. "She's standing right over there."

"Doesn't look much like a wine merchant to me," Bug grumbled.

"No . . . no, she isn't," Shem said. "But she has this son—the guy standing next to her—who is a rabbi or something. She heard about the wine running out, so she said that we had to do whatever her son told us to do."

"Weird," I replied. "So what did he say?"

"Well, we have these six big stone jars,"

Shem explained. "They hold, I dunno, twenty or thirty gallons each. The rabbi guy told us to fill them up with water."

"What? All of them?" Bug said.

Shem nodded. "Yeah. All of them. It took a little while, but we did it. And then he told us to scoop some out and serve it to the man in charge of the wedding."

"'Cause it wasn't water anymore. It was wine!"

"What? A cup of water?" I laughed. "I bet he was impressed."

"He was," Shem replied. And he looked dead serious. "'Cause it wasn't water anymore. It was wine!"

"So this rabbi guy turned water into wine?"

I looked at Bug. Bug looked at me. And we both laughed.

"So this rabbi guy turned water into wine?" Bug said. "What'd he do next? Pull a turnip out of your ear?"

"It happened. Honest! Just like I told you," Shem insisted. "I don't know how he did it. But

everybody here says it's maybe
the best wine they ever
tasted."

"So you don't
need our wine, then," I
sighed. "That's the point.
You didn't have to make up
some crazy story as an excuse."

"I didn't make it up!" Shem said. "Ask any
of the other servants. It was like a . . . a . . . miracle.
That's what they're all saying."

"Well," Bug grumbled, "it will be a real miracle if we don't get in trouble for losing this sale.
And all thanks to your wine-making rabbi guy."

Then he picked up one of the wineskins and
stamped off. And I stamped after him.

"It's Jesus," Shem shouted after us as we
stamped away. "I think the rabbi guy's name is
Jesus."

"Do you really think we'll get in trouble for
this?" I asked on the way back to the market.

"Nah." Bug grinned. "I just wanted to make
him feel bad."

"To bug him?" I said.

"Exactly!"

But Bug was wrong.

When we arrived, my dad was waiting for us. His arms were crossed. He was tapping one foot. And my brother had this really annoying smirky look on his face.

"So where have you boys been?" my dad asked. And not in a friendly "How's your day gone?" kind of way.

I looked at Bug. Bug looked at me.

And then, for some strange reason, Bug decided that retelling the story Shem had told us would somehow help.

Again he was wrong.

At the point where Bug reached full miracle mode, my dad put up his hand and shouted, "That's it! It's bad enough you took the wine without asking. Even worse, at that very moment, I was making a deal with a customer to sell him the wine you had taken. A deal that I have now lost. But the worst thing of all is to expect me to believe

"Because we all know how we feel about miracles in this family, don't we?"

some ridiculous story about rabbis and jars and miracles."

Then he stared at me. Hard. "Because we all know how we feel about miracles in this family, don't we?"

I hung my head.

My mom got sick. My dad prayed. She died.

So much for miracles.

"Good night, Bug," Dad said at last. And Bug didn't need telling twice. He slipped away with a wave and a sheepish glance.

"As for you, Gideon," Dad said, "there are animals that need seeing to."

So I put the wineskins back where I'd found them. And as my brother snickered and adjusted them just so, I went to the place where we kept the cages. And I fed the chickens. And the doves. And the goat.

Because that's all I am, I guess.

Goat Boy.

Chapter Two

WHERE ME AND BUG FIND A MESS OF FISH

We were in Capernaum. By the sea. It was a nice day. So Bug sneaked away from his dad's market stall and wandered over to ours.

"Hey, Bug," I said.

"Hey, Bug."

"Hey, Goat Boy," he replied. "I've got a brilliant idea! Why don't we go down to the docks?"

"Hey, Goat Boy."

To be honest, I didn't think it was that brilliant. The docks are okay, I guess, but not the most interesting place you could think of. And they smell like fish. Which is all right if you like the smell of fish. Which I don't. 'Cause it makes me retch.

"I don't know," I said. And I could tell that was not the answer Bug wanted. Mainly because he immediately started bugging me.

"C'mon," he said. "It'll be fun."

"Don't worry," he said. "We won't be gone long."

"And besides," he said. "We might get some free fish!"

Fish. That put me right off, but not nearly so much as the thought of having to listen to Bug bug me the rest of the day. So I said, "Yeah, all right."

But as we headed off, the annoying voice of my brother followed us. As usual.

"Where do you think you're going?"

Like I said, my brother's name is Sam, short

for Samson, who was known mostly for pushing people around. And seeing as my brother doesn't have any Philistines or temple pillars to push, he mostly just pushes me. Or tries to.

"None of your business," I shouted. Except that it probably was, seeing as Dad was away buying stock, and he'd left Sam in charge of the stall. And me.

But that was a detail I was willing to overlook, assuming I could get away. Which I did, because Sam had to stay there to keep people from stealing things. So all I heard, as I made my escape, was the familiar list of insults Sam always throws at me.

"Waste of space."

"Lazy."

"Good-for-nothing Goat Boy."

We took the long way to the docks, looking around the market, checking out stuff that we could never afford, and generally wasting time. Why not? It's what lazy, good-for-nothing goat boys do.

To be fair, we saw nothing that we hadn't seen a hundred times before. And I pretty much expected the same when we reached the seaside.

But that's not what happened. Not at all.

Bug was the first to see it. But I'm pretty sure I smelled it first. He ran ahead, right away, to get a closer look. And me? I stopped for a moment to try to keep my stomach from erupting.

What was it?

The biggest pile of fish either of us had ever seen.

Why did I stay? Why did I wrap my cloak around my face to block out the smell? Because it was amazing, that's why. Two empty boats, a gigantic pile of fish, and just one old man sitting there beside it, his head in his hands. And nobody else around, at all. But then it was late, way past the time when the fishing boats usually came in. Which made the whole thing even stranger.

"Hello, boys," he sighed. "What can I do for you?"

"The f-fish . . . ," Bug stammered. "How did you catch so many fish?"

"How did you catch so many fish?"

"Didn't catch them," he said matter-of-factly. "They were—how shall I put it?—*left* here."

"Somebody just left all these fish?" I said. "That's . . . that's . . . crazy!"

"My feelings exactly." The old man sighed. (He was doing a lot of sighing for a man with so many fish.) Then he looked us up and down. "Glad to see that at least some fathers have sensible sons."

"We're not that sensible," Bug admitted. "Really."

The old man shook his head. "More sensible than my boys. I can tell you that. One minute they're looking at more fish than they have ever caught in the whole of their lives. And the next minute, they're running off after some rabbi."

"A rabbi?" I asked. "Why?"

The old man shrugged. "From what I can gather, they think the rabbi had something to do with all these fish."

"I thought rabbis were people who taught about God," Bug said. "What do they know about fishing?"

The old man smiled. For the first time. "A sensible boy." He nodded. "Sensible enough to see that rabbis know *nothing* about fishing. So when this rabbi says to my boys' partner, Simon, that he should cast his nets in the middle of the morning, when no sensible fisherman fishes, what should Simon have done?"

"Umm . . . the sensible thing?" I guessed.

"Exactly!" The old man beamed. "He should have told the rabbi to find his own boat if he wanted to go fishing so bad. In the middle of the morning. When all the fish are at the bottom of the sea."

"He didn't do that, then?" Bug asked.

"He did not," the old man said. "He has a history with this rabbi, does Simon. Well, they all do. So he did what the rabbi asked. And with the help of his equally unsensible brother, Andrew, he set sail with the rabbi and cast his nets into the sea."

"And caught all of this?" I said, pointing at the fish and gagging just a little.

"So many fish," the old man replied, "their nets began to tear. They had to call for my boys, James and John, to bring their boat to help them. And still, there were so many fish that they only just made it back before the weight of it all could sink their boats."

"But . . . but it doesn't make any sense," Bug

said. "Catching all those fish in the middle of the day."

"No sense at all," the old man said. "But it happened. You can see for yourself."

And smell it, I thought.

"I reckon it was just beginner's luck," the old man said. "But my boys and their friends think God and that rabbi, Jesus, had something to do with it. So they've left me and gone to follow him. To be 'fishers of men.' That's what they told me. Which makes no sense to me at all."

"So they've left me and gone to follow him. To be 'fishers of men.'"

Wine out of water. Fish out of nowhere. It sort of made sense after all.

I looked at Bug. He looked at me. We'd heard about Jesus before. In Cana, at the wedding.

Wine out of water. Fish out of nowhere. It sort of made sense after all.

Still, I felt sorry for the old man. I really did.

But the smell of all those fish was literally making me sick, so I looked again at Bug and gave him a kind of sign like I thought it was time to go.

But Bug had a different kind of look in his eye. A look I'd seen before.

When Bug's dad is about to make a brilliant deal, he gets an excited, slightly crazy look in his eye. And that's the look Bug had.

"So what are you gonna do with all these fish?" he asked the old man.

"Dunno." The old man shrugged. "We have people we usually sell to. I say 'we,' but it's just me now. And that's the problem. My sons used to do all the running around and delivering and dealing with the merchants. It's too much for one old man to do alone. That's why I'm sitting here. I'm just trying to figure out what to do next."

Bug smiled. "Well, I have a very . . . sensible suggestion. My friend . . . umm . . . Gideon, here, and I work for a couple of excellent market traders who would gladly take these fish off your hands. For the right price, of course."

I couldn't believe it. Bug actually sounded like he knew what he was doing. Like a proper businessman. Like his dad.

The old man smiled back at Bug. "I think that's a very sensible idea," he said. "Run and fetch your business associates, and let's see what kind of deal we can do."

So that's what we did. We ran to the market and talked our dads into going back to the docks with us. To be honest, I was kind of worried about the idea. The thing with the wine hadn't gone well at all. And I wasn't sure they would even take a look. But they did. And when they saw the fish, they were as amazed as we were. And yeah, Bug's dad immediately got that look in his eye.

They bought the fish at a knockdown price 'cause the old man just wanted to get rid of them. Then they sold them at a fat profit to everyone they knew.

Bug's dad was happy with us, and my dad was happy with us. And I was happy too, even though I lost my lunch a few times during the delivery process.

But it was worth it, particularly when we got back to the stall that night, exhausted.

Sam had stayed behind to watch things, and when we arrived, he said to me, in his snarky way, "So I guess you're proud of yourself, then?"

"Nah," I said back, "I was just doing what any lazy, good-for-nothing goat boy would do."

Or maybe, for the first time, somebody who was more than just a goat boy. A proper businessman, maybe. Like his dad.

WHERE ME AND BUG BREAK STUFF

Life's not fair. Sometimes you get in trouble for doing exactly the kind of thing grown-ups do.

Take my dad.

Yeah, he can be strict. And grumpy. And

I guess a lot of that comes down to my mom being gone. But he can be really nice, too.

I mean, if there's some poor person who wants to buy something from his stall and doesn't have enough money, sometimes he gives them a break.

Not always. But sometimes. It depends.

Bug's dad thinks that's nuts. "You take care of your family and your business first." That's what he says. But I think he's just maybe more interested in money than my dad.

Anyway, we were still in Capernaum. Which is by the sea. Which is very nice. And we were staying with my uncle Micah. Which is not so nice.

But that's what we do when we travel around the country. We either stay with family (and we have lots of family!) or we stay with friends my dad has made over the years.

Uncle Micah is . . . was . . . my mom's brother. And everybody says he's really smart. He went to a special school and learned a lot about the laws of our religion.

I don't know what he's talking about half the time, but people seem to listen and nod their heads like he's really clever. Or maybe they're just trying to keep themselves awake.

Anyway, this one morning, he went on and on about how he was going to see this new rabbi everybody was talking about.

"You can't be too careful," he explained in his teachy, I-know-more-than-you-do voice. "There are a great many individuals who pass themselves off as authorities on the matter of our laws and traditions, but who, in reality, know nothing about them whatsoever."

He uses a lot of words, my uncle Micah does. Most of which sound a bit like blah-blah-blah-blah to me. But then he said a word—a name, actually—that got my attention.

"The rabbi? Jesus. Jesus of Nazareth."

I tapped my dad on the shoulder. He brushed my hand away.

I whispered in his ear, "Dad." He shushed me.

I jumped up and down a bit, like I needed to pee.

And that did it.

"I believe the boy is in some discomfort," Uncle Micah said. "It might be best to escort him from the room."

Escort me from the room? Really?

"I don't have to pee," I said. Red faces all around.

"Whiz?" I suggested.

Dad's face in his hands. Sam muttering, "Idiot."

"Be escorted from the room?" I said at last. And that seemed to do the trick. "It's just that I saw that guy, Jesus, once—in Cana, at a wedding. He turned water into wine. At least that's what one of the servants told me."

Dad gave me that hard stare of his again. Then he turned to everyone else and said, "I'm really sorry. We have already had a little talk about this."

Uncle Micah waved one hand like he was chasing away a fly. "No need to apologize. There have been rumors of this sort running round Galilee. Water into wine, as the boy says. A leper cleansed. A woman healed. I hasten to add that I have not personally observed any of these so-called miraculous events, nor have any of my colleagues. That is why we are so keen to meet this rabbi and hear what he has to say. I understand that teachers like myself will be coming from as far away as Jerusalem to see the man, today. I will give you a full report upon my return."

Then he rose and headed for the door, opened it, and looked at me. "Perhaps I should take a jug of water with me." He laughed. "And have the rabbi turn it into wine for our evening meal."

I didn't think that was very funny.

My dad didn't either, but for a whole different reason.

"You made us look foolish," he grunted as we made our way to the market. "It's hard enough, what with your uncle being so clever. And me just a market trader. And your mom . . . well, your mom really admired him. And . . . and . . . that's why it's important not to say foolish things. All right?"

I wanted to tell my dad that I didn't think Uncle Micah was actually all that smart.

I wanted to tell him that I didn't think there was anything wrong with selling stuff for a living.

I wanted to tell him that I was sort of proud of him.

But Sam was behind us snickering and really enjoying all the trouble I was in, and I figured if I said anything he'd just make fun of me.

So I grunted back an "Okay" and kept my head down.

I fed the goat and the chickens. The doves had all been sold. And that's when I heard Bug shout, "Hey, Goat Boy!"

"Hey, Bug!" I shouted back. "What's up?"

"Need a hammer. And I need it now."

"Why? Did something break?" I asked.

"Hey, Goat Boy!"

"Hey, Bug!"

Bug grinned. "Nope. Something needs breaking!"

Then he just kept grinning. Which I knew meant he wanted me to ask him what, exactly, needed breaking. Which I wasn't going to do because he would then ask me to go and break whatever it was with him. Which I didn't need to do, seeing as I was in enough trouble already.

But he was so desperate to tell me that, yeah, he started jumping up and down like *he* needed to pee.

"All right," I sighed. "What needs breaking?"

"A roof!" he replied, like it was the most exciting answer ever.

"I'm not lending you a hammer to bust up somebody's roof," I said. "My dad would kill me if he found out."

Bug grinned again. "But what if I told you that it was *my* dad's cousin who needed it?"

"Why would one of your cousins want to break up a roof?"

More grinning. "Because he wants to help

his friend. You know, Cousin Saul, who we're staying with?"

I nodded. "I know."

"Well, Cousin Saul has this friend, Benjamin, who can't walk. So he and three of his other friends decided to carry him on his mat to see Jesus. You know, the rabbi guy who did the wine thing and helped that old man's sons catch all those fish? Seems he's still in Capernaum."

"They say people have come all the way from Jerusalem to hear him."

I nodded again. "I know."

"Problem is, there's no room in the house where Jesus is staying. They say people have come all the way from Jerusalem to hear him."

I nodded a third time. "I know."

"You know a lot. For a goat boy," Bug said. "But I bet you don't know this. Because there was no room in the house, my cousin and his friends carried Benjamin up onto the roof, where they are, at this very minute, about to tear it open and lower Benjamin in!"

I shook my head. "That I did not know."

"So how about that hammer?"

I weighed it all up. Doing something nice for someone—my dad would do that. So why wouldn't he be pleased if I helped? Particularly if there wasn't much chance of him finding out.

"Okay," I agreed. And then I went over to my dad and said, "Bug's cousin needs to borrow a hammer for a bit. He needs to . . . umm . . . fix something. All right if I help?"

Luckily, he and Sam were attending to customers.

"Sure," Dad muttered. "Just get back as fast as you can."

I followed Bug to the house, and

yeah, it was packed.

There were loads of people hanging around outside, still trying to get in. Jesus was obviously a very popular guy.

We didn't hang with them, though. We crept up the steps on the side of the house, right onto the flat roof. And sure enough, there was Bug's cousin and three other men, and Benjamin, lying on a mat.

"Thanks, Goat Boy!" Bug's cousin said. He had a big smile on his face, and I knew I'd done the right thing.

Each of the men had a hammer now, and they started banging the tiles loose, then pulling them up.

Bug and I helped too and dragged the broken tiles to one side. In no time at all, there was this huge hole in the roof, big enough to lower their friend through. I was really happy for them.

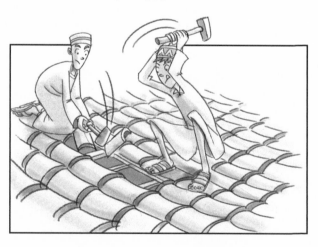

And then I caught sight of Uncle Micah.
Or rather, he caught sight of me. And suddenly
I didn't feel so happy.

At first, there was this surprised look on his
face. But it turned into an angry look real quick.
Everyone else in the room was pointing up at
us, but he was pointing down and mouthing the
words, *"Get off! Now!"* For once, I had no trouble
understanding what he meant.

But I wasn't getting off the roof, either. I had
to get Dad's hammer back, for a start. But I was
also really interested to see what would happen.

Bug's cousin and his friends carefully lowered Benjamin to the floor. Jesus didn't seem to
be bothered by that at all. But then it wasn't his
house, I guess.

I whispered to Bug, "What do you think he'll
do now?"

"Dunno," Bug said. "Say some magic words?
Wave his hands around?"

Jesus paused for a minute. He scanned the
room. Then he looked down at Benjamin, lying
on his mat. "My friend," Jesus said, "your sins are
forgiven."

Bug's cousin scratched his head. "I'm

"Your sins are forgiven."

confused," he said. "Don't we want him to fix his legs?"

His friends seemed confused too. But Uncle Micah? Uncle Micah was so angry that he looked like he was going to explode. And the other teachers around him weren't any better. They started grumbling and muttering among themselves.

So Jesus turned to them. "I know what you're thinking," he said. "You're thinking that only God can forgive a man's sins. And you're thinking I have insulted God by claiming I can do it too. So let me ask you a question. What's harder? To forgive a paralyzed man's sins or to make him walk?"

I looked at Bug. Bug looked at me.

"They're both kind of hard," I whispered.

"Like turning water into wine."

Bug grinned.

"Here's what I'm going to do," Jesus continued. "To show you that I have the power to forgive this man's sins, I will fix his legs."

"Pick up your mat. Walk!"

Then he looked down at Benjamin again and said, "Pick up your mat. Walk!"

And you know what? He did!

The place went crazy. Bug's cousin and his friends were whooping and hollering and jumping up and down so much that I thought they might fall through the hole themselves.

> The place went crazy.

The people in the house were just as excited. They moved aside so Benjamin could walk out the door, and they followed him, praising God and stuff.

Not everyone was happy, though. Uncle Micah and his bunch were huddled in a corner, not one smile among them. They looked angry and worried and a little afraid.

I figured it would be better if I explained all this to Dad before Uncle Micah did, so I grabbed the hammer and ran down the steps.

And wouldn't you know it, Dad was standing right there. And he wasn't happy, either.

"Where have you been?" he shouted. "I told you to come right back. I've been looking all over for you."

"I'll tell you what he's been doing," said Uncle Micah, who wasted no time in joining us. "He's been up to no good. That's what. He's been on the roof of this house, tearing off the tiles! Add that to his ridiculous antics at breakfast this morning, and . . . well, all I can say is my sister would be none too pleased with that boy's behavior."

Dad looked down at the hammer in my hand. "Young man," he said, "if that is true, you are in a whole load of trouble."

See what I mean? You try to do something nice. You do what you think your dad would want you to do. And still you get in trouble.

And I almost did. Except, at that exact moment, Bug's cousin came rushing down the steps and slapped my dad on the back so hard, it nearly knocked him over.

"Thanks for the hammer!" he said.

"You got some boy, there!" he said.

"He was a big help. You ought to be proud of him!" he said.

He told my dad everything that happened— with the roof and Jesus and Benjamin, who couldn't walk and who could walk again now. Then he rushed off, following the happy crowd.

"Well, yes, there was the healing," Uncle Micah said. "Assuming, of course, the man was actually paralyzed in the first place. You can never tell. Particularly when Jesus used the healing to say some very unusual—dare I say blasphemous—things."

Dad looked at Uncle Micah. It was like he was looking at someone he'd never seen before. Like he was seeing something new. Something he didn't like. "We both know how I feel about miracles," he replied. "But as far as my boy goes, it seems all he was doing was trying to help somebody. I can't see anything wrong with that. And I don't know why you should, either."

Then he put his hand on my shoulder and led me back to the market.

We stayed with a different relative that night.

WHERE LUMP HATES BEANS

It was the worst day of the year.

> We had to stand around in a really long line.

> We had to stand there for ages.

> We had to carry stuff that just got heavier the longer we waited.

And we had to listen to everybody moaning and groaning and complaining. Especially my dad and Bug's dad, who complained louder than anyone.

"I hate tax day," grumbled Bug's dad for like the twenty-seventh time.

"A waste of effort and a waste of money," grumbled my dad.

"Because where does the money go?" grumbled Bug's dad.

"To the Romans!" grumbled my dad.
And everyone around us booed and hissed and grumbled too.

"That's right, the Romans," added Bug's dad—who, like any good market trader, loved it when people listened to him. "The ones who conquered our land. And kill our people. And treat us like slaves. And then expect us to pay for it."

There was more booing and hissing and grumbling, until this huge Roman soldier with a huge spear marched up to us, a huge hand on his huge sword. And then, suddenly, everything went real quiet.

Like I said, it was the worst day of the year.

This year it was even worse. But not

because my brother, Sam, was picking on me again. He was back minding the stall.

This year it was even worse.

No, it was worse because Bug's cousin Lump was in the line with us.

It's not that I don't like Lump. It's just that he sort of drives me crazy 'cause he's not really like anybody else I know.

Bug's mom calls him things like *different* and *unique*, but I just think he's kind of weird. Not bad weird. Just *weird* weird.

I mean, we were standing in the line, right? Everybody was miserable. And what was Lump doing? He was sitting on the ground. Making little sculptures. Out of dirt and mud and sticks. With little round sheep-poo eyes!

"Here's a lovely chicken," he said, holding it in front of my face. "I made a donkey too. And a goat, just for you."

What was I supposed to do? Stick it in my bag? Hold it in my hand? It was made of poo!

To be fair, it did look exactly like my goat, which was amazing, really. Yeah, all right, unique.

"I'm bored," Bug yawned.

"I'm bored too," I yawned back.

"I'm ten, nearly eleven," Lump said.

See what I mean?

"Dad?" Bug bugged. "Could we maybe just run around for a while? It'll be ages till we get to the tax booth. The line's hardly moving."

"No," Bug's dad grunted. "You need to stay in this line and suffer with the rest of us. How else will you learn to hate the Romans as much as we do?"

"But I already hate the Romans," Bug said. "Honest."

"I hate them too," I added. Anything to get out of that line.

"I hate beans," Lump said.

"How about this?" my dad suggested. "The boys can run around until we are, say, ten people from the front? Then they get back in the line again."

"We might need all of it to pay our bill, particularly if that tax collector is feeling greedy today."

"But who's gonna carry the stuff they're holding?" Bug's dad asked. "You never know. We might need all of it to pay our bill, particularly if that tax collector is feeling greedy today."

"One of them can stay and hold it," my dad said, "while the other two run around."

"That's not fair!" Bug bugged again.

"We'll draw straws for it," my dad said. "Shortest straw stays."

"All right, then," Bug sighed. "It's better than nothing."

But it wasn't better, not for Bug anyway, when he drew the short straw.

And I suppose it wasn't better for me,

either, when I realized that I had to run around
with Lump.

"Beware!" he shouted, the piece of straw he
drew dangling from his nose. "I am an evil dragon
and I will devour you."

Then he chased me, away from the line and round and round the square, roaring and waving his arms.

It was kind of embarrassing, actually.
I thought it was never going to end, but then he
ran into an old lady who swung her bag around
to keep her balance and knocked the straw right
out of his nose.

"My apologies, madam," he said, taking her hand. "But you have rescued me from the curse of the dragon, and I will be forever grateful."

I thought she would whack him again. But instead, she just smiled and walked away.

Guess she thought he was "unique," too.

"Listen, Lump," I said. "Maybe we should do something else. Watch the fishermen or play on the beach or something like that."

"I want to watch the tax collector," Lump said.

"Why? You heard what my dad and Bug's dad said. Everybody hates him."

"And I said I hate beans," Lump replied. "But that doesn't mean everybody hates them."

"Right. Okay," I said, scratching my head and wishing I had drawn the short straw. "Well, how about we go and watch the tax collector and then maybe go to the beach after that?"

Lump grinned. "Excellent! And then you can eat beans and I can be a sea monster."

And we can all live in Weird Town, I thought.

We wandered up to the tax collector's booth and stood a little way off, at the side, watching. We were just a couple of kids. Nobody paid

"I wonder what will happen."

any attention to us or seemed to care that we were there.

"I wonder what will happen," Lump wondered.

"It's not that interesting, really," I told him. "I've been here, with my dad, a couple of times before. The tax collector is the man in the booth. His name is Levi. The people come up to the booth, like that man there. He tells them what they owe, and then they pay him."

"With money?" Lump asked.

"Sometimes with money. Sometimes with stuff they have—pots, jewelry, animals . . . anything that's worth something. Look, that man is handing over a couple of chickens."

"Poor chickens," Lump sighed. "They are going to a new home. With the tax collector and his wife and his two children, I think. A boy. A girl. Maybe two boys. I don't know. Will the chickens be happy there? Will they make a new life for themselves? It's hard to say. I'm glad I'm not a chicken."

"I think they'll probably just go to the Romans. Or get sold," I said. "And I don't think you have to worry about them. They're just chickens."

"Nobody is just a chicken," Lump replied.

I was sort of wishing Lump would stop talking and go back to making his sculptures, when one of Levi's enormous bodyguards grabbed hold of the man who had handed over the chicken and started shaking him. The poor guy was so scared that he handed over the rest of his chickens and some other stuff too.

"See that?" I said. "That happened to my dad once. He paid what he owed, but the tax collector wanted more. Dad didn't want to get beat up, so he just gave him what he wanted. That's why he hates tax day so much. You never know how much you're gonna have to pay. You're pretty much at their mercy."

Lump shook his head. "Just like chickens."

I was trying to think of something to say to that—something sensible, maybe—when somebody I did not expect to be there walked up to the tax collector's booth.

"Do you see that man there?" I said to

Lump. "His name is Jesus. He made a paralyzed man walk. I saw it with my own eyes. And he turned water into wine."

Lump looked at Jesus. He stared at him for ages.

"I don't think he hates beans," Lump said at last. "And I am absolutely certain he cares about chickens."

I scratched my head. Again, I was not quite sure how to respond. So I just motioned to him and we crept a little closer.

"What do you think will happen?" Lump whispered.

"Levi works for the Romans. He takes more than he should. He makes people's lives miserable. But Jesus works for God, right? He's a rabbi. He heals people. He does good things. So I think he's going to tell that tax collector off."

That was not quite how it went.

"Levi," Jesus said, "I'm looking for disciples who will learn from me all about God's Kingdom. I want you to be one of those people. Come, and follow me."

Levi looked at Jesus. He looked at the

"Come, and follow me."

crowd. He looked at his big bodyguards and the pile of money he had collected. Then he stood up, left his booth, and walked away with Jesus.

Everybody was shocked. And then, once they realized that they wouldn't have to pay their taxes (at least until another tax collector showed up), they cheered.

I didn't know what to make of it all. And I said so.

"Why would somebody like Jesus want somebody like Levi to follow him?" I wondered.

"He loves beans," Lump said. "That's why."

And then Dad showed up. He was happy. And Bug's dad was happy. And even Bug seemed happy. And why wouldn't he be? He hadn't been hanging out in Weird Town.

"Don't know about water and wine, or paralyzed guys," Dad said, "but Jesus performed a real miracle today—taking on that tax collector and trying to turn him round. Good luck to him, I say."

Then Bug's dad snapped his fingers. "I have just had a brilliant idea. This Jesus seems to gather crowds wherever he goes. Why don't we follow along and set up our stalls in the places he goes to? We'll have ready-made customers everywhere!"

Dad nodded. "I think you're onto something there. We'll keep our ears to the ground and find out where he's going."

"But we're going to need more help to deal with all those crowds," Bug's dad said. Then he snapped his fingers again. "I've got another great idea. Lump, how would you like to come with us and help?"

"I would be delighted!" Lump said. Then he held out one of his sculptures. "Can I bring my sheep along?"

Bug rolled his eyes.

And I sighed.

My future was clear.

Keep up with Jesus.

Make a pile of money.

And spend loads of time in Weird Town.

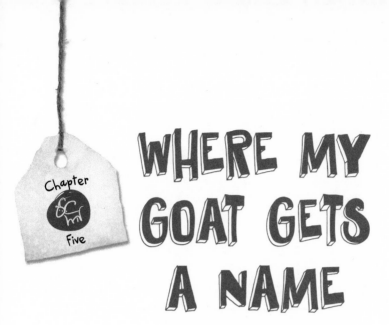

WHERE MY GOAT GETS A NAME

"So what does this make you, then?" My big brother snickered. "Less-Than-Goat Boy? I-Lost-My-Goat Boy?"

"I tied her up like I do every night!" I said. "I don't know what happened. Maybe the rope

broke. Maybe somebody took her. But it wasn't my fault!"

"You still lost her," Sam sneered. "And that's all that matters. She's your responsibility, so you have to go and find her."

"But it's the Sabbath!" I said. "We're not supposed to work on the Sabbath. And I'm pretty sure that wandering all over the place, looking for a lost goat, counts as work."

"On the contrary, my younger and seriously misinformed brother," Sam replied. "I have been in contact with our esteemed uncle Micah, and he informs me that seeking out and saving an animal in peril is one of the exceptions to the rule. Sorry."

He wasn't sorry at all. And the fact that he was starting to talk like Uncle Micah made me even more annoyed. But what could I do? I was stuck. So I set off to find our goat.

We were staying with Dad's cousin Eli now, and his house backed onto a bunch of barley fields. I figured if the goat went anywhere, she went out there to find something to eat.

It seemed like a good place to start. And then Lump arrived. And things were suddenly sort of less than good.

"I heard you lost your goat," Lump said. "It must be heartbreaking."

"Well, it's not great," I said. "And I'll be in big trouble if I don't find her. But I don't think I'll have a broken heart or anything."

Lump reached into his bag and pulled out one of his animal-poo sculptures. "I know I would be heartbroken if I lost little Lily here."

"That's a very nice model of a camel," I said. "And I like what you've done with those poo-ball eyes. But I don't feel the same way about the goat."

"Everybody needs help sometimes."

"Well, I will help you find her anyway," Lump said.

"No. No, you really don't have to. I lost her. It's up to me to find her."

"I insist," Lump insisted.

"Everybody needs help sometimes. Jonah needed help when he was in the belly of the fish. Daniel needed help when he was in the lions' den. And my uncle Ezra needed help when he accidentally swallowed a bowl full of tadpoles."

"Sounds awful," I said.

"He was burping up frogs for months," Lump said. "So let me help you. Please."

Yeah. Weird Town. I know.

"All right," I sighed. "I thought I'd start looking in this barley field."

We had only taken five steps into the field, however, when Lump asked another question. "What's the name of your goat? It might help if we called out her name."

"The name of my goat?" I replied. "My goat doesn't have a name. She's a goat."

Lump frowned. "Everybody needs a name."

"But she's not an every*body*," I said. "She's a goat."

"Well," Lump said, "every *goat* needs a name."

I shook my head. "No, every goat doesn't! As my dad has told me more times than I can count, goats are for milking and selling and, eventually, eating. That's why you don't name them. So you don't get attached to them."

"Well, that explains everything," Lump said. "Your goat left because she didn't feel loved."

"Look, I fed her, I watered her, I took care of her. Love has nothing to do with it. She's a goat!"

Lump stopped and crossed his arms and looked at me. "You did your duty," he said. "But there is so much more to taking care of animals than doing your duty."

"How would you know?" I shouted. "The only animal you have is made of poo!"

"And mud. And straw," Lump corrected me. "Molded together with love. And that's how you should have taken care of your goat."

"Well, she doesn't have a name! Okay? So we're just going to have to look for her."

"We could give her a name," Lump

suggested. "Goatser. No, Miss Goaty. No, Penelope. That's it! We'll call her Penelope."

> "That's it! We'll call her Penelope."

"But if I never called her that before, why would she come to me if I called her that now?"

"Because we'll do it with love! Penelope! Dear Penelope! Everyone responds to love."

I was about to say something very non-loving to Lump, when he pointed and said, "Look, there's that Jesus man."

I turned around, and Lump was right. Jesus was walking through the barley field, and a bunch of other guys were walking with him. Levi the tax collector was there, so I figured the rest were probably his disciples too.

They were laughing and joking, and every now and then, they would stop, grab some barley, rub the grain back and forth in their hands, and then eat the kernels inside.

Lump tried it too. "Mmm. Good," he said.

We watched them awhile, and then we saw a group of men coming from the other direction.

"Get down!" I whispered. "It's Uncle Micah

and some of his friends. Don't know what he's doing out here, but he sort of has it in for me. He'll find some way to get me in trouble for being here, I know it."

"He'll find some way to get me in trouble for being here, I know it."

We peeped through the barley as one of Uncle Micah's friends walked straight up to Jesus.

"Harvesting grain, I see?" He sneered. "You do know, of course, that harvesting grain counts as work, and that working on the Sabbath is a violation of our laws. What do you have to say to that, Jesus?"

"Here's the thing," Jesus said. "You are experts in the Law, so I am sure you have read what happened when our ancestor King David was hungry. He and his men went into God's house and ate the bread that was only supposed to be eaten by the priests.

"Mercy, not ritual."

"You see, God gave us the Sabbath to meet people's needs, not so we could keep a set of rules. Remember what the prophets said? Mercy,

"I am the Lord of the Sabbath!"

not ritual. And anyway," Jesus said, a twinkle in his eye, "I am the Lord of the Sabbath!" Uncle Micah and his friends went nuts. You couldn't actually see the smoke coming out of their ears, but you could tell they were really angry.

"There he goes again!" Uncle Micah grumbled. "Acting like he's somebody special. Acting like he's God himself!"

Then they all stormed away, leaving Jesus and his friends to finish their barley lunch.

"So what did you think of that?" I said to Lump. But when I turned around, he was gone.

Great, I thought. *Now I have to look for* him *too.*

And that's when I heard the *naa-naa*-ing.

"Here you go, Penelope," Lump said, my lost goat following happily behind. "There's a good girl. Here's your Goat Boy. He has promised me that, from now on, he will call you by your name and treat you with love, and not just because it's his job to take care of you."

Then he looked at me.

"All right, I promise." And then—this is the honest truth—she licked him and she licked me, and we went back to the house together.

Me.

And Lump.

And, yeah, Penelope.

Chapter Six

WHERE LUMP NEARLY LOSES A FRIEND

Business was good in Capernaum.

Bug's dad was convinced it all had to do with what he was now calling the Jesus Effect.

My dad wasn't so sure. But Jesus was still around, healing and teaching and stuff. And there did seem to be bigger crowds than normal. Which meant that I was now allowed to serve customers, in addition to my goatly duties.

Bug was really busy too. And Lump? Lump was working out great, according to Bug's dad. Apparently old ladies in particular really liked him. Some of them had even bought his sculptures. Ick.

Ick.

This one morning, while I was feeding the animals, Bug and Lump showed up.

"Lump needs to borrow Penelope," Bug said.

"I have this friend who is sick," Lump explained. "I thought it might cheer him up."

I scratched my head. "Why would seeing a goat cheer somebody up?" I asked.

"Because Penelope is a lovely goat," Lump said. "Seeing her would cheer *me* up. And because I can't really think of anything else."

"All right," I sighed. "Where does your friend live?"

"Not far," Lump said, untying the goat. I mean, Penelope. I was still getting used to the name thing. "Follow me."

We walked for what seemed like ages.

"I thought you said it wasn't far," Bug moaned.

"It's not far now," Lump said. "We just have to turn down this street, and . . . there it is: the centurion's house."

"The what?" Bug shouted.

"The centurion's house."

"You do know what a centurion is?" I asked.

Lump nodded. "A Roman army commander."

"And you do know that we hate the Romans, right?" Bug said. "That they conquered our land and kill our people and treat us like slaves?" He sounded exactly like his dad.

"I do know that," Lump said. "But I also know that this is a nice centurion."

"No such thing," Bug grunted.

"I have been friends with his servant boy, Crispus, for two years, and the centurion has always been kind to me. He says he likes Jewish people, and he even paid his own money to build the big synagogue in the middle of town. I think maybe he's different from other Romans."

"I don't care how different he is," I said. "We're not really supposed to hang out with people who aren't Jewish."

"Maybe somebody should tell that to them," Lump said, pointing at a bunch of very important men—Jewish men—who were banging on the centurion's door.

The centurion opened his door to speak

with them; then they rushed away as quickly as they had come.

"C'mon. If it's okay for them, then it's okay for us."

So the three of us, and Penelope, walked up to the centurion's house. And Lump knocked on the door.

A servant lady answered, then turned and called, "Master, it's Crispus's friend. The Jewish boy. You know, the one who's a little . . . different?"

Lump beamed. "Did you hear that? Looks like the centurion and I are both different!"

Bug rolled his eyes.

If only you knew, I thought.

And then the centurion came to the door.

I don't think I had ever been so close to a Roman before, not even on tax day. He was tall and proud and had these enormous muscles. He looked like someone who was used to being in charge. He was, in fact, everything that Bug's dad and my dad hated about Rome.

But when he bent down to speak to Lump, all that changed. There were tears in his eyes.

"I brought a goat to cheer up Crispus," Lump said.

The centurion forced a smile. "I'm very sorry, my boy, but you won't be able to see Crispus today. He is very, very ill. There is nothing more that the doctors can do for him. So the elders of your people have kindly agreed to find a healer called Jesus and ask him to make Crispus well. He is our only hope. Thank you for your concern. I'm sure Crispus would appreciate it." And he shut the door.

Lump stood there, staring at the door.

Then he wiped one eye with the back of his hand and ran off in the direction the elders had gone.

"Lump, where are you going?" I shouted.

"To find Jesus," he called back.

"To find Jesus."

I looked at Bug. Bug looked at me. Penelope *naa*-ed.

"Guess we should go after him," Bug said. So we did. We looked down alleys and around corners. And I think I even saw Penelope sniffing the ground like she was a search-and-rescue goat.

In the end, though, Lump wasn't actually that hard to find. The news about the elders and the centurion had spread all over town, and all we had to do was ask a couple of people where Jesus was, and they pointed the way.

The crowd was gathered in the market. There were the elders. There was Jesus. And there was Lump.

But by the time we got to him, the crowd was already heading back our way.

"Jesus is going to do it," Lump said. "The elders told him what a nice Roman the centurion was and asked him to heal my friend. And Jesus said he would!"

"So we're going back to the centurion's house?" I said.

"Where we just came from?" Bug moaned.

Lump grinned. "Yup!"

We passed our market stalls on the way. I thought we might be in trouble, but my dad and Bug's dad and Sam were so busy taking care of customers that they didn't even see us.

It would have been hard, though, even if they had been looking. It was like we were part of a giant parade, there were so many people. I couldn't believe it.

And then, suddenly, everybody stopped.

Well, everybody but Lump.

"I'm going up front," he said, "to see what's happening."

And yeah, we went with him, slipping between legs and bumping into a big butt or two along the way.

"He believes all you have to do is to say the word, and his servant will be healed."

When we finally got to the front, we saw another group of people approaching Jesus and the elders.

"We are friends of the centurion," they announced. "He has sent us to tell you that he does not feel worthy to have you visit his house. He says that, as a Roman officer, he understands what it means to be in command. He tells his men what to do, and they do it. No questions asked. So in the same way, he believes all you have to do is to say the word, and his servant will be healed."

"He has faith that I have seldom seen."

Jesus turned to the crowd. He looked surprised. He looked happy. "Did you hear that?" he said. "This centurion is not even one of our people, yet he has faith that I have seldom seen."

Then he turned back to the men and said, "Tell the centurion that his servant will be healed."

Lump jumped up and shouted, "Hooray!" Then he ran after the men who had come from the centurion's house, with Penelope prancing behind.

"Should we stop him?" Bug asked.

"What's the point?"

So we just wandered along to the centurion's house and waited until Lump eventually came out.

"It's like there was never anything wrong with him."

He was smiling his *unique* smile again. So we figured his friend was all right.

"It's like there was never anything wrong with him," Lump said. "And he loved meeting Penelope. I knew she would cheer him up."

"Now that you mention it," I mentioned, "where exactly is Penelope?"

And that's when the door opened again.

"Excuse me . . . young man," a servant girl called. "You seem to have left your . . . goat . . . behind. I don't suppose you could come back and fetch him?

We can't stop him chewing on the bedcovers."

"Be right there!" Lump said. He turned to us and chuckled. "Now that is different."

"No argument here," I said.

Lump shook his head and grinned. "No, I mean that servant girl—she thinks that Penelope is a *boy.*"

WHERE WE WALK FOREVER AND END UP AT A FUNERAL

We had been on the road for ages.

"Where did your dad say we were going?" I asked Bug.

"He didn't say." Bug shrugged. "He got the word that Jesus was leaving Capernaum. He saw all the people who were leaving with him. And he decided to put his Jesus Financial Strategy into operation."

"So that's what he's calling it now?" I asked.

Bug laughed. "Yeah, it gets fancier the more he thinks about it. He's absolutely convinced if we set up shop wherever Jesus goes, it will make him a rich man."

"If it doesn't kill the rest of us first," I sighed.

"A killing." Bug chuckled. "That's exactly what he wants to make. Why do you think he loaded our carts with food? Because he's hoping the trip will be long enough that everyone else in the crowd runs out of grub, and they have to come to us."

Bug's dad got his wish. The trip went on and on. And the farther we went, and the more we stopped, the better business got.

"What did I tell you?" he shouted to my dad, over the hubbub of hungry customers. "This Jesus thing is a gold mine!"

Dad had to agree. "Best idea ever!" he shouted back. "It's working so well, in fact, that I think we might be running out of bread."

"Cut them in half, then," Bug's dad suggested. "No, cut them into strips. That'll make the bread stretch further. And . . . and . . . we'll serve them with a piece of dried fish. How about that?"

Then he turned back to the crowd and shouted, "Fish and strips, everybody! Get your fish and strips!"

Personally I was just glad for the rest. We were serving customers, yeah, but at least we weren't walking.

"Fish and strips, everybody! Get your fish and strips!"

And then, just like that, we were. I raced around to get our chickens back in their cage and loaded on the cart. I gave the donkey a swat to get moving, then scratched Penelope's head, and we ran to join the others.

"What's the rush?" I said when I caught up to Bug. "We don't even know where we're going. Why are we in such a hurry to get there?"

"Dunno," he said. "But you know my dad's rule."

"We go where Jesus goes, yeah," I groaned.

"I think it would be nice if we could fly," said Lump, who had been unusually quiet up to that point.

"Dream on," Bug grunted.

"No, really," Lump said. "I have been working out the plan carefully as we walked along."

Aha! I thought. *That explains the silence.*

"You would need a very big cart," he explained. "Because lots of people would want to go. And even then, you would probably have to squeeze them in and it would still be uncomfortable."

Bug nodded. "Right. Big cart. Uncomfortable seats."

Lump went on. "Then, because you would

be up in the air, there would be a lot of swooping and diving to miss clouds and mountains and birds. And a lot of getting blown around by the wind. All that moving around could make people want to vomit, and because the seats were so close together, you wouldn't want them to vomit on each other. So you would need bowls to catch the vomit."

Bug nodded. "So—big cart, uncomfortable seats, and vomit bowls."

"That's right," Lump said. "And then you know how it is after you vomit. Sometimes you want a little water or something simple to eat. Nothing fancy to upset your stomach again. Just something plain and unappetizing."

"So, big cart, uncomfortable seats, vomit bowls, bad food," Bug said. "That's the future of traveling as you see it?"

"That's it!" Lump beamed.

"Sorry to disappoint you," Bug said, "but I don't think it's ever going to fly." And he laughed.

"Because it's a birdbrained idea." I laughed back.

Lump sighed. "So what you're saying is you don't think it will ever get off the ground?"

He paused. And then his eyes lit up. And as we laughed, he said, "Hey, I made one too!"

And then the laughing stopped.

"Settle down, boys!" my dad said. "We're coming up to a town, and it looks like there's a funeral procession coming our way."

Ever since my mom died, my dad has been pretty fussy about funerals. You have to show respect.

"It's really noisy," Lump said.

"That'll be the professional mourners," I said.

"Professional what?" Lump asked.

"Mourners," Bug answered. "You know,

people who cry and wail and tear their robes in grief. For money."

"What a strange job," Lump said.

"So you've never been to a funeral?" I asked.

Lump shook his head. "No. I don't think so."

"Yes, you have!" Bug said. "You were at Great-Uncle Ephraim's funeral. I was there too!"

"That was a funeral!? I thought it was his birthday party."

Lump scratched his head. "That was a funeral? I thought it was his birthday party."

"He was lying there, dead!" Bug said.

"Hmmm . . ." Lump shrugged. "I figured he was just tired. He was always a quiet man."

"If you boys don't settle down," my dad threatened, "there is going to be trouble."

My big brother, Sam, snickered. Of course. And me and Bug and Lump shut up.

When the funeral procession reached us, we could see everything. The dead person was a young man. He was lying in a box that was carried by some other men. And the saddest crying was coming from a lady, standing right with them, who looked like she could be his mom.

I tried to stand as respectfully as possible, but it was hard not to be upset by her crying. I glanced up at my dad. He was finding it even harder.

"Don't cry."

Then, suddenly, the crowd on our side of the road parted, and Jesus walked through. He went right up to the lady and said to her, "Don't cry."

I thought my dad was going to explode. He turned redder than I have ever seen him. And then, through clenched teeth, he said, "What right does he have to say that to a grieving mother? He ought to be ashamed."

But Jesus didn't stop there. He walked over and laid his hand on the coffin.

"That's it!" Dad said, turning his back. "Your miracle worker has gone too far. That is about the most disrespectful thing he could do. Challenging a woman's grief. Stopping a solemn procession. I have had enough of this!"

And he stomped away in anger.

So he sort of missed seeing what happened next.

Jesus looked at the guy in the coffin and said, "Young man, get up."

> "Young man, get up."

And there, right in front of us all, that's what he did. He sat up and he started talking.

It was freaky and scary and just plain weird, at first. And more than a few people fainted. Including my brother, Sam.

There was some confusion, as well, at least from one person.

"So is this how most funerals end?" Lump said. "Because if you ask me, it really is a lot like a birthday party."

> "No, this is definitely not how most funerals end."

"No, this is definitely not how most funerals end," I said.

"So the young man was just sleeping, like Uncle Ephraim?"

Bug sighed. "Uncle Ephraim was not sleeping. He was dead. And this guy was dead too."

Lump pondered. "So then that means Jesus . . . brought him back from the dead!"

"Exactly!" Bug said.

"Which is even more amazing than a flying cart!" Lump said.

"Just a bit," I said.

Once people got used to the idea, though, they started cheering and praising God and thanking Jesus.

And seeing as everyone was now in a cheerful mood, yeah, Bug's dad opened for business.

He did it without my dad, though, who was off by himself, sitting on the ground, his head hanging between his shoulders.

I stood next to him for a while, and when he didn't tell me to go away—or say anything at all—I sat down.

"You heard what happened?" I asked.

"Hard to miss," he grunted.

"So Jesus wasn't being disrespectful," I said.

"No." Dad sighed. "Just unfair."

I didn't have to ask what he meant, but he said it anyway.

"I'm happy for that mother and her son, but why? Why them? Why not your mother? Why not us? Why does God bless some families and leave others to live with nothing but their grief?"

"I don't know, Dad," I said. Because I didn't.

So I just sat there with him till the crowds had gone, and the shop was closed, and everyone was getting ready to leave again.

"C'mon, Gideon," he said at last, climbing to his feet. "There's no point staying here, is there? Time we joined the others."

So we did. We headed down the road. A road, I hoped, that would take my dad to a better place.

WHERE A GIRL HITS BUG WITH A ROCK

"Did you see that?" Bug said.

"See what?" I said, too busy to look his direction. Dad and Sam were away, talking with suppliers. So I was helping customers. At last!

"That girl punched me," Bug said. "Her mom

was paying for a couple of bowls, and she came around the side of the stall and punched me on the arm."

"Then you must turn the other cheek," said Lump, who was working on one of his sculptures. A lion, I think.

"What cheek?" Bug said. "She punched me on the arm."

"Then turn the other arm." Lump rolled a bit of something between his fingers—I didn't want to know.

"What are you talking about?" I asked.

"Jesus," Lump said. "We have been following Jesus around, right? So I've been listening to what he has to say. And he says that if somebody hits you on one cheek—or arm—you should not hit him back, but turn the other cheek—or arm—so he can hit that too."

"That is the stupidest thing I ever heard!" Bug said. "You'd just end up with two bruised arms—or cheeks—instead of one."

"Well, that's what he said." Lump shrugged. "Thought you'd like to know."

"Well, I don't," Bug moaned. And then he shouted, "Hey!"

"What now?" I said.

"That girl. The same one. She's standing over there, making faces at me!"

"Blessed are the peacemakers," Lump said. He was working on the mane now. "That's what Jesus says."

"What?" Bug grunted.

"Perhaps you have hurt that poor girl and that's why she is punching you and making faces at you. Maybe it's time to make peace with her."

"I don't know her!" Bug cried. "I just met her. Just now. How could I have done anything to hurt her?"

"Dunno," Lump said. "Just thought it might be helpful."

"It might be helpful if you kept all that Jesus stuff to yourself," Bug muttered.

"No," Bug's dad said. "It might be helpful if you all stopped yapping and did your jobs. There are some ladies at the end of the stall who need assistance. Money doesn't grow on trees, you know!"

"Actually," Lump said, "your Father in heaven knows what you need, even before you ask. He dresses the flowers like Solomon and he feeds the birds. How much better, then, will he take care of you?"

"What's he going on about?" Bug's dad said.

"Apparently," I replied, "Lump went to listen to what Jesus had to say."

"Well, it might be fine for Jesus to dress like a bird and eat flowers, but we live in the real world. And in the real world you have to fight for every scrap."

"Actually," Lump said, "that's not exactly what he said."

"Actually," Bug's dad replied, "I don't care what he said. We're not following him because we need to be enlightened. We're following him because it's good for business. And for business reasons that I have yet to understand, people seem to like your little animals. So get to work! And as for you," he continued, pointing at me, "there are still customers waiting at the other end of the stall!"

I didn't need telling twice (well, I guess I did), so I went to help them.

They seemed real nice. They were talking like they were friends. And they were dressed like they had lots of money. Which was strange, seeing as we usually sold stuff to more ordinary people. And which was not so strange, 'cause it explained why Bug's dad was so interested in them.

"We couldn't help but overhear," one of the ladies said, "but did you say you were following Jesus?"

"Umm . . . well," I said, "we have sort of been going where he goes. I almost saw him turn water into wine. And I did see him heal a paralyzed man. And bring a boy back to life."

"Is he the Messiah or not?"

"So what do you think?" one of the others asked. "Is he the Messiah or not?"

"The Messiah?" I asked.

"You know," a third lady said. "The Savior that God has promised to send us, for years and years."

"Umm . . . well," I said again. "I don't really know. I mean, Jesus does some amazing things, I guess."

And then a rock came zipping past our heads, followed by a shout.

"She hit me with a rock!" Bug shouted. "That girl! She hit me with a rock!"

The ladies and I looked, and yeah, there was a girl—eleven or twelve maybe—waving at Bug and grinning. Then she disappeared into the crowd.

"Love your enemies."

Bug clenched his fists and got set to run after her.

"You're going nowhere, mister," Bug's dad said, clamping a hand on his son's shoulder.

"And besides," Lump added, "what good will it do if you return evil for evil? Love your enemies, I say, and do good to people who persecute you."

"How about if I persecute *you*?" Bug muttered.

But one of the ladies started to clap. "Now there's somebody who has been listening to Jesus! That's really something."

I rolled my eyes. "Something unique. Lots of people say that about him."

"But that's what's so interesting about Jesus," she replied. "It's not just the healings. It's also what he says. He really does want everything to be as God intended—to see God's Kingdom here on earth. And that's why his teaching sounds so foreign to the way we usually live."

"Like new wine in an old skin," Lump said,

putting the finishing touches on his lion.

"Sorry?" I said.

"Your friend really *has* been listening!" the third lady said. "That's a phrase Jesus uses to show how unusual and new and different his teaching is."

"He really does want everything to be as God intended— to see God's Kingdom here on earth."

And that's when

another rock zipped past.

And knocked over—and broke—a jug on the stand.

"It was that girl again!" Bug shouted.

"Now she's gone too far!" Bug's dad growled. "You can hit my boy with a rock, but you'd better not hit my stuff." And he started to leave the stall.

"Now she's gone too far!"

"Wait, wait," one of the other women said.

"This is a perfect example of how things can change when you react differently."

Then she turned to Bug. "Why do you think that girl is pestering you?"

"Dunno," Bug said. "And it's more than pestering. It hurts!"

"Speaking as a woman," spoke the woman, "did it ever occur to you that she might be doing it because she likes you?"

"Likes me? Ickkk! Umm. No," Bug said, looking really confused.

"Well, that is a possibility," the woman said. "We girls do have our ways of getting attention."

Bug was still trying to get his head around this. I couldn't tell if he was happy with the idea or not. I was just glad it wasn't me!

"Why don't you go over there and say hello," the lady suggested.

Bug shook his head. "Nah. Couldn't."

"Probably better than another rock," one of her friends said. "And why not take her something?"

"Like a lion!" Lump said, handing over his sculpture.

Bug's dad sighed. "Beats losing another pot,
I guess. Go on. Take it to her.

So Bug reluctantly took the lion and walked
toward the girl. When he got halfway there, he
looked at us over his shoulder. I have never seen
him so worried.

The girl backed away at first. Then she
walked up to Bug, and they started
talking.

"But seek
first God's Kingdom
and his righteousness,
and all the rest will be
taken care of too."

"See?" one of the ladies
said. "Problem solved."

"Yeah, but who's
gonna pay for that
pot?" Bug's dad said.

"Don't ask
what you will eat or drink,"
Lump said. "But seek first God's
Kingdom and his righteousness, and all the rest
will be taken care of too."

"What? Even pots?" Bug's dad asked.

"If that's what you need," one of the ladies
said. And she handed Bug's dad a coin. "Consider
it done."

"But you don't have to do that!" Bug's dad
said. "You didn't break it."

"We don't have to give money to Jesus and his disciples, either," one of them answered. "But we do. Because we think he could very well be God's Messiah. And because that's one of the ways God works—and takes care of the people who trust him."

And then they left.

And Bug's dad scratched his head. "Well, I'll be . . ."

And Lump smiled and made a little model bird. Sitting on a flower.

WHERE I FIND OUT BUG'S REAL NAME

Chapter
Nine

Bug's dad grinned at my dad. "Business is good, yeah?"

"Yeah." My dad nodded.

"So we stick with the plan, yeah?" Bug's dad said.

Again my dad nodded. "Yeah. We go wherever Jesus goes."

"You just have to look at these crowds!" Bug's dad said. "Jesus is in town. You can hardly move! We'll make a fortune here. You'll see."

He was right. There were people every-where. And then one particular person walked out of the crowd and up to the stall. It was Bug's new friend.

"Hey, Rock Girl!" I said.

"Hey, Goat Boy!"

I call her Rock Girl 'cause she was, you know, the girl who threw rocks at Bug. Her real name is Beckah, which is okay, I guess, but not nearly so good as Rock Girl.

And hey, everybody else has a nickname, so it's only fair.

"How you been?" Bug asked.

Rock Girl shrugged. "Not that great, actually. I was pretty sick last night. Sweaty. Shaky. Fevery."

"Pukey?" Lump asked.

Rock Girl nodded. "And pukey. Very pukey."

"What about the other end?" Lump inquired.

Me and Bug both winced. "Ick! Lump!"

But Rock Girl didn't even blink.

"*And* the other end." She grinned.

See, here's the thing. My dad says Rock Girl is "bigger than life," whatever that means. All I know is she's fun, and she likes hanging out with us, and she's not grown-up at all, for twelve, and not really all that girly. So she's all right with me.

"You feeling better?" I asked.

"You're quite the gentleman, for a goat boy," she replied. And I did not blush. I promise.

"Ick!"

"You're quite the gentleman, for a goat boy."

"And I am better," she said. "Much better, thank you. Because when I woke up this morning, I discovered that a very special guest was staying at my house."

"Was it a cat?" Lump asked. "I dreamed I was a cat once."

Rock Girl smiled. "It was not a cat. It was a person. Specifically, it was Jesus!"

"Really?" I said.

"Really." She nodded.

"And I really was a cat," Lump added. "I didn't just dream it. I think. It's hard to remember. I was asleep for most of the time."

"So how did that happen?" Bug asked.

"Not sure," Lump said. "All I know is that when I woke up, I really wanted to eat a mouse."

"Not you!" Bug shouted. "Her!"

Rock Girl smirked. "Well, as you know, my father is in charge of the synagogue. A very important job. And since Jesus is quickly becoming a very important person, too, it only made sense that he should come and stay with us."

Did I mention that my dad also thinks Rock Girl is kind of spoiled and full of herself? I have no idea where he gets that.

"But here's the best thing," she went on. "He's giving a little talk at our house today. And my father says that the three of you can come to the house and see him."

"Excellent!" I said.

"Sounds okay to me," Bug said.

"Will there be any cats there?" Lump asked.

"Only in your dreams," Rock Girl laughed. And she grabbed him by the arm. "C'mon!"

We slipped through the alleys and down the streets. And when we finally arrived at Rock Girl's house, nobody had to point and say, "There it is!" because there were people everywhere, trying to get in.

"Move over. Out of the way! Synagogue Ruler's Daughter coming through!"

"Move over. Out of the way!" Rock Girl shouted. "This is my house. Synagogue Ruler's Daughter coming through!"

Her dad must have been as important as she said he was, because everyone moved aside, and me and Bug and Lump followed behind.

Just as we were about to reach the door,

though, Bug tapped me on the shoulder and pointed.

I ignored him. I was trying to keep up with Rock Girl.

So he tapped me on the shoulder again. Harder this time.

I didn't want to lose sight of her. And I wasn't in the mood to be bugged. I ignored him again. So he punched me.

"What?" I shouted.

"Look!" he shouted back. "That lady over there. We saw her at that wedding, remember? That's Jesus' mom."

I looked, and yeah, she did sort of seem to be the same lady. But it didn't make any sense. If she really was Jesus' mom, why was she outside and not in the house with him? I know Rock Girl thought *she* was important, but I figured Jesus' mom was kind of important too. In spite of his bugging, Bug had to be wrong.

Rock Girl squeezed through the crowd huddled at the door. We squeezed in behind her. She waved to a man sitting near Jesus. He gave a little wave back and smiled. It had to be her dad. Jesus was already talking, so we plunked down in the first space we could find.

Jesus talked about lots of stuff, which would probably have been a lot more interesting if Lump, our designated Jesus fanboy, hadn't kept interrupting.

"Oh, this is a good one."

"You'll love this next story."

"I bet you can't guess the ending."

Just as I was about to tell him to cut it out, though, someone near the door called out across the room.

"Jesus! Your mother and your brothers are here. They want to see you."

Bug gave me this *see, I told you so* look.

And Jesus just went quiet for a bit. Then he looked at his disciples. Then he smiled. "Who is my mother? Who are my brothers? These are my mother and my brothers." And he pointed around at everyone who'd come to listen to him.

"Whoever does what my Father in heaven wants them to do—those are my mother and sisters and brothers."

"Who is my mother? Who are my brothers?"

He said a couple more things after that. But it didn't take very long. Then he got up and left, his disciples following behind. And most of the crowd, behind them.

"I'm kind of confused," I said.

"Me too," Lump agreed. "I thought we were going to see some cats."

"No," I sighed. "I mean the thing about his mother and brothers. Okay, sometimes I wouldn't mind having a different brother. All right, most of the time. But I really miss my mom. What he said seems kind of rude, that's all."

Bug looked out the window. "Well, he's

hugging his mom right now. And she's hugging him back. So I don't think she thought it was rude."

Just then, somebody cleared his throat. It was Rock Girl's dad.

"Hello, Father," Rock Girl said. "These are my new friends."

"Very pleased to meet you," he said.

"Me too," I replied. I think that was the right response. Although it also sort of sounded like I was happy to meet me too. Oh, well.

"Pleased to meet you too," Bug said. Much better, I thought.

"Sorry you don't have any cats," Lump said. Worse. Much worse.

But Rock Girl's dad just carried on, as if Lump hadn't said anything weird. He was obviously a very polite man. Or hard of hearing. "I couldn't help but overhear your conversation."

Not hard of hearing, then.

"And I think I might have an answer to your question."

Lump raised his hand.

I pulled it back down again. "Our question about Jesus' mother and brothers," I said.

Lump looked disappointed.

Rock Girl's dad nodded. "Yes. That's right. As my daughter may have told you, I am in charge of the synagogue. People come to the synagogue to worship God, to pray, to learn about him. Over time, they get to know each other pretty well, and they become a kind of family. No, they are not all related by birth, but because they share the same goals and ideals and interests, they look upon each other as brothers and sisters—sometimes even more than they do their physical brothers and sisters. I have a lot of respect for Jesus, and I think all he was trying to say was that people who dedicate their lives to doing what God wants, much as he has, are like family to him."

"They look upon each other as brothers and sisters— sometimes even more than they do their physical brothers and sisters."

The explanation was a bit long-winded, I thought, but it made sense. I didn't want another long explanation, though, so I just nodded and said, "Thanks."

Bug did the same.

But Lump? Well, Lump was Lump. And

before I could stop him again, he said, "A bit like Bug, then?"

And Bug went white.

"Because Bug's adopted, right?" Lump went on. "And even though he wasn't my cousin when he was first born, he is really a part of my family now."

Bug was fiery red, and I was glad I was sitting between him and Lump.

"I'm not sure Bug wanted everyone to know that," Rock Girl's dad said.

Rock Girl put her arm around Bug in a sympathetic sort of way. And I felt something I hadn't felt before. Annoyed, maybe? Or maybe something else.

"It's okay," Bug sighed. "I guess you all would have found out sometime." Then he glared at Lump. "Well, the rest of you, anyway."

"So you don't know who your real parents are?" I asked.

Bug shook his head. "Nope. I was left at the stall one day, when I was just a baby. It's before your dad and my dad started working together, so I don't think even he knows. My mom and dad took me in. They didn't even know what my name was. But my mom said I was 'cute as a bug,' so that's what they called me. And it stuck."

"So that's why you never told me your real name?" I said. "Because your real name actually is . . ."

"Bug." He grinned. "And I'm sticking with it. Because as annoying as Lump is, he's right. They might not be my flesh-and-blood family, but they are my real family, no matter what anybody says."

So it all sort of worked out all right, in the end, I guess.

Lump didn't get punched.

But he did get disappointed again, when Rock Girl's dad asked us to stay for dinner and Bug and me said we had to get back to the stall.

And I did get annoyed again, for some reason, when Rock Girl gave Bug a good-bye hug and told him how brave she thought he was.

What about me? I thought. *I'm brave. I have to put up with my stupid non-adopted brother every day of the year.*

Anyway, at least I got the solution to one of my life's mysteries.

My friend's nickname was Bug. And strange as it may seem, his real name was too.

WHERE MY BIG BROTHER TOSSES HIS COOKIES

"I like drinking water," Bug said. "I like looking at it too. And splashing around in it when I'm hot. But I'm not that crazy about the idea of floating on it. Across the sea. All the way to the other side."

"Well, it's your dad's idea, not my dad's."

GOAT STEW:
1 innocent Penelope
1 hin of water . . .

I shrugged. "He's the one who wants to follow Jesus wherever he goes. I don't think my dad's too sure about crossing the sea, either. We had to leave the animals with my relatives. Penelope wasn't happy at all. And it doesn't help that my aunt's favorite recipe is for goat stew."

Bug glanced down the shore. "Well, that's definitely Jesus and his guys climbing into a boat. So I guess we're pretty well stuck."

"Stuck with what?" Lump asked, dumping a load of stuff into the boat.

"This crazy seafaring adventure," Bug grumbled.

"And what an adventure it will be!" Lump beamed. "The fresh breezes. The gentle waves. The smiling mermaids. I can't wait."

"Not sure about the mermaids," I said.

"Oh, you'll love them," Lump said. "From what I hear, they are very friendly." Then he giggled. "And pretty."

"No, what I mean is that I don't think they actually exist."

Lump thought about this for a minute. "But who will save us from the sea monsters, then?"

"Actually . . . ," I began.

Bug shook his head. "Leave it. There's no point. He'll only bring up something else. Like mer*men* or something."

Lump's eyes lit up. "Mer*men*? There are mer-*men*? I had no idea. Then *they* will fight the sea monsters. I can't wait!"

And off he went to grab another load.

"At least someone's happy," Bug said.

But Lump might have been the only one.

As we loaded the boat, my dad argued with Bug's dad about the whole idea.

"We don't even know where Jesus is going," he said. "There might not be any towns or customers there at all!"

"There are customers everywhere!" Bug's dad insisted. "New markets. Fresh fields. We just have to be willing to take the chance."

And as for my big brother, Sam, he was looking green at the thought of even climbing onto the boat.

"Okay there, Big Brother?" I asked. "Feeling a little . . . queasy?"

He shook his fist at me, but that's all he had the strength to do. Maybe this little voyage was going to be all right, after all!

We waited for Jesus and his crew to set sail, and then we set off too.

"Keep your distance," Bug's dad instructed the man who owned the boat. "But be careful to keep them in your sights."

So that's what he did. And with Lump looking for mermaids on one side, and Sam tossing his cookies off the other, we began our journey.

We traveled for a while. And everything was going smoothly. Gentle breeze. And gentle waves too.

"Not too bad, so far," Bug said, even though he was still holding on to the side of the boat pretty tightly.

"I think Sam's finally gone to sleep," I said.

"Nothing left to hork," Bug said. "But Lump looks a little disappointed."

And yeah, he did. There was, sad to say, a definite lack of mermaids and sea monsters.

The man who owned the boat sat down next to Lump. "What you looking for, me boy?" (He had a strange, sailor way of talking.)

"Unusual sea creatures," Lump said.

"Aaar, well, you be sitting in the right place fer that." (He also used strange sailor grammar.)

"Really?" Lump said.

"Aaar!" The sailor nodded. (And why he used the letter R so much was a complete mystery.) "I seen many a strange thing on these waves."

"Mermaids and sea monsters?" Lump asked, excited again.

"Aaar! That and more!" the sailor said.

I couldn't believe it. He was actually encouraging Lump.

"I seen waves big as 'ouses, and the shapes of all kinds of creatures swimming under them."

"But they could have been fish, right?" I asked.

"They coulda been anything!" he roared. "The sea is a strange and cruel mistress. She does what she likes. There is no understanding her. No controlling her. She swallows whom she will and spits out their bones on the briny shore."

"She swallows whom she will and spits out their bones on the briny shore."

Lump's eyes kept getting bigger and bigger. And his smile kept growing too.

Bug, meanwhile, was getting paler and paler and hanging on to the side of the boat with every bit of strength he could find.

And all I could think was that, somehow, Bug's dad had managed to hire the craziest captain on the Sea of Galilee.

And then, suddenly, he didn't seem that crazy at all.

The sky went gray and scary. The waves turned gray too. And that gentle breeze became a fierce wind.

Soon the boat was rolling forward to back and side to side, all at the same time.

The waves kept getting bigger and nastier

and before long they were not only crashing against the side of the boat, but splashing into it as well.

"Hang on, me hearties!" the sailor shouted. ("Me hearties?")

But there was no need to tell us, really. We were already doing that. For dear life!

My dad and Bug's dad were trying to keep both themselves and the stuff we'd brought from washing overboard.

Sam had somehow managed to find even more vomit to add to that mix.

Bug had his eyes shut. I think it's just possible that he might have been praying.

The crazy captain was doing everything he could to keep us afloat.

"Woohoo!"

And Lump was having the time of his life.

"What an adventure!" That's what he kept shouting. That and "Woohoo!" Like he had no idea we could drown at any minute.

And then he shouted something else. "Look! Look! Out on the sea. There's a figure rising up. It's a mermaid. Or a mer*man*. I knew it!"

The captain looked too. "Aye, the lad's right. There be something out there the likes of which these old eyes have never seen."

The waves were splashing in my face. It

was all I could do to hang on to the boat. But I looked too. And yeah, there was something out there that definitely looked like a someone. A person. But it couldn't be a mermaid or a merman. Could it?

And then a voice echoed out across the storm. A voice that cut through the wind and the waves.

"PEACE! BE STILL!"

A voice that I recognized at once.

And when the wind stopped blowing, just like that, and when the waves stopped crashing, just like that, and when everything was bright and calm again, we could all see who the voice belonged to.

"Aww, it's just Jesus standing in his boat," Lump sighed. "Not a merman at all."

"Just Jesus?" I said. "*Just* Jesus? He stopped the wind blowing and calmed down the waves and probably saved our lives. What do you mean, *just* Jesus?"

> "Well, when you put it that way, it was pretty amazing."

Lump shrugged. "Well, when you put it that way, it was pretty amazing."

"*Pretty amazing?*" the captain said. "Why, that were the single most incredible thing I ever seen in all me time at sea! That feller's no myth of the briny deep, no shadowy figure beneath the waves. We seen it with our own eyes. That feller's fer *real*! Aaar!"

The other thing that was for real was that a whole bunch of our stuff had been washed away. So in spite of the fact that we were alive, my dad and Bug's dad were still pretty upset. Or maybe it would be fairer to say that my dad was still pretty upset with Bug's dad.

"I know it looks bad," Bug's dad said. "But when we get to the other side, we'll sell everything that's left to the crowds that are waiting for Jesus. And then we'll just buy new stock. It'll be fine. You'll see."

Except that it wasn't.

It's not that the rest of the trip was bad. It was just fine.

It's not that Sam kept vomiting. He didn't.

And it's not that we lost sight of Jesus and his boat. We stayed right behind, careful to keep it in sight.

No, the problem was with where we landed.

Oh, there were plenty of bodies, all right.

It's just that they were all dead.

Chapter Eleven

WHERE LUMP CHASES A GHOST

"We crossed the sea and risked our lives for this?"

My dad stood in the boat, his hands on his hips, disgusted. "We crossed the sea and risked our lives for this?" he grumbled.

Bug's dad scratched his head. "I have to admit, it's quiet."

"Because it's a cemetery!" my dad shouted. "And last time I checked, dead people make really lousy customers!"

Lump raised his hand.

"Lump," I whispered, "this is probably not the best time."

"Are you sure?" he whispered back, wandering dangerously close to Weird Town. "I just thought it might be helpful to remind your dad that there are probably some ghosts running around, and we could sell to them."

"Absolutely, definitely not the best time," I said.

"The thing is," Bug's dad said, back in Sensible Conversation Land, "where there are dead people, there must be live people too. We just have to find them."

My dad sighed. He looked up the coast one way. He looked down the coast the other way. "Do you see any live people? Apart from us, of course. And Jesus and his friends, who seem to have disappeared round the bend, down there."

"Well, no," Bug's dad said. "Not here, of course. But up on top of the hill there, I'm sure there must be a town or a village or something."

"Then why don't you go up there and have a look?" my dad suggested. "Before we unload what goods we have left in this boat and waste even more time."

Lump put up his hand again. "I really think I should tell him about the ghosts."

"I really think you shouldn't," I replied, pulling his hand down again. "Dad's not in a very good mood."

I think Bug's dad realized that too. So he went off without any further argument, taking Bug along for company.

Dad sat down on the beach, fed up and frustrated.

The crazy boat captain looked all around his vessel for any signs of damage.

And Sam, who was still a little green, crept over to join me and Lump.

"Hello, Vomit Boy!" I said.

Sam made a fist. "When I feel better . . ."

"You don't scare me," I said. (And he didn't. Well, not then. He still looked kind of pukey.) "And besides, Lump says we have scarier things to be afraid of than you. Things like ghosts."

Lump raised his hand a third time. "I didn't

actually say *scary*," he reminded me. "Just that there were ghosts and they might like to buy something. I'm not sure if all ghosts are scary or not."

Sam sneered. It was a sickly sort of a sneer, but a sneer nonetheless. "Hasn't anyone ever told you that there are no such things as—?"

Sam would have finished the sentence if he hadn't fainted.

But then I nearly did too at the sound of the inhuman shriek that came, at that very moment, from somewhere in the graveyard.

"Ghosts!" Lump cried, leaping out of the boat and running off into the cemetery. "Woohoo!"

"Better go after him," my dad sighed.

"You wouldn't want to?" I asked.

"Nope." He sighed again. "I just want to sit here and ponder my sad and desperate business position."

I turned to Sam. Oh yeah. Wouldn't do much good to ask the Unconscious Kid.

> The farther I went, the creepier it got.

So I hopped out by myself and went after Lump, running through a maze of tombs. The farther I went, the creepier it got. And when I finally caught sight of him, things got creepier still 'cause he was running after somebody else— a screaming, shrieking somebody with chains hanging from his arms and legs!

It could have been a ghost, I guess. But it just looked like a crazy person, or an escaped criminal, maybe. And that made me even more worried for Lump.

"Lump!" I shouted. "Wait!" But I don't think he could hear me over all the screaming. Then he tripped and fell behind one of the tombs. And the crazy chained-arms-and-legs person kept running.

"You all right, Lump?" I said, out of breath, when I got to him.

"Sprained my ankle, I think." He gri-
maced. "Where's the ghost?"

I stuck my head round
the tomb. "You're not gonna
believe this. It looks like he's
headed straight toward Jesus."

"Come out
of this man, you
unclean spirits!"

Jesus looked at the crazy
chain guy and shouted, "Come out
of this man, you unclean spirits!"

And the freakiest, scariest voice I ever
heard came out of the chain guy. It wasn't even
one voice. It was loads of voices. High voices and
low voices and men's voices and women's voices
all screaming together. "Jesus, Son of God on high!
What do you want with us? Do not torture us,
please!"

I was terrified. And even Lump looked like this was no longer some kind of exciting adventure. That poor guy was filled with loads of evil spirits. And it didn't help that we were still more or less in the middle of a graveyard.

But Jesus didn't look scared at all.

"What is your name?" he asked the evil spirits.

"My name is Legion, for there are many of us! Please don't send us into the abyss," they screamed. "Send us into the herd of pigs!"

Lump and I looked around.

"There!" Lump pointed. "The pigs are on the hill, over there."

Jesus nodded, and just like that, the man collapsed in a heap and lay there without moving a muscle. But the pigs? The pigs went wild!

They started squealing and stampeding. There must have been thousands of them! Then they rushed down the hill and ran right into the sea in a horrible, squealing, splashing, drowning mess.

"Poor pigs," Lump whispered.

I was about to say they were just pigs, but I knew how Lump would feel about that, and anyway, I sort of felt sorry for them too. They were just minding their own business, doing what pigs do.

The good news, though, was that the crazy chain guy didn't look crazy anymore. Some of the disciples had helped him up, and now he was just sitting there, all normal, talking to Jesus and his disciples.

"Guess we ought to get out of here," I said to Lump.

And then things went sort of crazy again.

A whole bunch of people ran down the hill where the pigs had been. They didn't head for the sea, though. They ran right up to Jesus. Some of them must have been the people who owned the pigs, 'cause they acted really angry. But when they saw that the crazy guy wasn't crazy anymore, they got really freaked out and begged Jesus to go away.

I figured it was a good time for Lump and me to go away too. So I lifted him up and helped him limp back to the boat.

When we got there, Sam had unfainted, though he looked like he might keel over again any second. And Bug and his dad were just coming back from their search for customers.

"There is a town on top of that hill," Bug said, "and while we were walking around, there was this massive pig stampede."

"I know," I said.

"And the pigs ran—"

"Right into the sea. We saw it—me and Lump. And here's something I bet you don't know. It was Jesus who made it all happen."

Then I told Bug all about the crazy chain guy, who was a normal chain guy now. Though I figured he probably didn't need the chains anymore, but it was easier than calling him the used-to-be-crazy, used-to-wear-chains guy.

"I'm really sad I missed that," Bug said.

Lump sighed. "The sad thing is that we didn't actually see any ghosts."

"No," Bug's dad said, "the sad thing is that the people in the town are all up in arms and not in the mood for traders from across the sea."

"No," my dad said, "the sad thing is that this entire trip was a waste of time and money."

"No," the boat captain said, "the sad thing be

that the skies be threatening, so we best be sailing back this minute, if not sooner. Aaar."

"No," I said, looking at my big brother, "the sad thing is that someone has to make another sea voyage."

"No!" Sam said.

And then he tossed his cookies.

Chapter

Twelve

WHERE ROCK GIRL GETS SOMETHING BETTER THAN STEW

When we got back from our crazy sea voyage, everybody was pretty miserable.

My dad was still angry with Bug's dad about wasting all that time and money.

Bug was still annoyed that he'd missed the crazy chain guy.

Lump was still moaning about not seeing any ghosts.

The captain was still complaining about the damage to his boat.

And my brother, Sam, was still tossing his cookies.

And me? I was just miserable because everybody else was. And a little worried about Penelope too.

Then we saw the crowd gathered by the harbor.

"Unload the boat, boys!" Bug's dad shouted as we hit the shore. "There's money to be made!"

My dad was suddenly a lot happier too.

And we, sort of, had to be happy along with them. Even though it was a lot of work!

We grabbed what stock had survived the trip, tugged and lugged it out of the ship and onto the shore, then set up a makeshift stall as fast as we could.

The cause of the crowd was not hard
to guess.

"There's Jesus!" Lump said.

No surprises there.

"And Rock Girl's dad," he added.

I looked up. I figured Rock Girl would be
there too. But she wasn't.

"Rock Girl's probably with her mom or
something," said Bug, who was obviously looking
for her too.

But Lump, as ever, just said the
first thing that came into his head.
"I bet she's there. We just can't
see her." And off he ran to look
for her, with my dad and Bug's
dad and Sam (of course) shouting
after him.

"There's work
to be done!"

"Hey, where are you going?"

"Get back here!"

"There's work to be done!"

Lump ignored them. Again, no surprises
there. But to be fair, he wasn't much use at the
stall anyway, except for making his little animals.

When he came back, he was all out of
breath.

"Rock Girl's sick," he said. "All sweaty and fevery and pukey . . . and the other way. Just like last time. But I think it must be worse."

"What do you mean?" Bug asked.

"Her dad looked really worried," Lump replied. "And he asked Jesus to come and help."

I didn't like the sound of that. If we had learned anything from following Jesus around, it was that he was the last hope of really hopeless people. Like the couple at the wedding who ran out of wine. Or the paralyzed man who got lowered through the roof. Or the widow whose son died. Or the crazy chained-up guy.

So if Rock Girl's dad was asking Jesus for help, then maybe he was hopeless too. And that wasn't good.

"Gotta go!" I said as I went. And I ran into the crowd so quickly that I didn't even hear what my dad shouted. I was willing to deal with that later. And I guess Bug and Lump were, too, because they were right behind me.

Jesus wasn't hard to find. We just had to follow the crowd. When we caught up with him, he was about halfway to Rock Girl's house. And he had stopped.

"What's he doing?" Bug asked me. "If Rock Girl's really sick, he needs to get there as soon as he can."

"Somebody touched me," Jesus said, which didn't seem to me like a good reason to stop. There were people everywhere!

And that's exactly what one of his disciples said. "Master, there are people pushing in all around us. What do you mean, somebody touched you?"

"It wasn't just that somebody bumped me," Jesus explained. "It was like they reached out to me for help. I felt God's power going out of me."

"Okay, okay," Bug muttered so only we could hear. "You helped somebody. Great. But there's somebody else who needs your help too. Let's get going!"

But it wasn't that simple.

This woman came forward.

"I've been ill for twelve years," she said to Jesus. "With a horrible, horrible disease. And I've spent all my money on doctors."

Hopeless again, I thought.

"But when I touched the cloak you're wearing," she went on, "I was healed!"

Everybody was amazed. But then some men pushed through the crowd and walked right up to Rock Girl's dad. And they didn't look amazed at all. They looked really, really sad.

"But when I touched the cloak you're wearing, I was healed!"

"We're so sorry," they said. "There's no need to bother Jesus any longer. Your daughter has died."

I couldn't breathe. It was like somebody had punched me in the stomach. Everything stopped. Rock Girl was . . . dead? I could feel the tears running down my cheeks. My nose was running. Bug was rubbing his eyes. And Lump was just sobbing.

It wasn't fair. Just like my dad said. Jesus healed all kinds of people. He healed that woman he didn't even know. But he'd stayed at Rock Girl's house. So why didn't he hurry? Why didn't he heal her? My friend?

"Trust me. Your daughter will be fine."

Jesus looked at Rock Girl's dad. He put a hand on his shoulder. "Don't be afraid," he said. "Trust me. Your daughter will be fine."

I didn't know what to think. But seeing as I was sort of one of the hopeless ones now, I didn't really have any choice but to follow them and see what happened. I looked at Bug and Lump and shrugged, and they shrugged back. Red-eyed, we walked with the crowd to Rock Girl's house.

We could hear the mourners wailing, long before we got there, and that didn't help anybody's mood.

"Wish they'd just shut up," Bug grumbled.

But they didn't. It was their job, after all. Which made me mad, in a way. They didn't even know her. How could they cry for her?

When we got to the house, Jesus started to go in with three of his disciples and Rock Girl's mom and dad. Nobody else was allowed to go with them.

As they entered, Rock Girl's dad saw us. He nodded like he was saying hello or sorry or something. I don't know.

And then Jesus said something really strange to everybody that I still don't understand.

"The girl's not dead. She's just sleeping."

"Don't cry. The girl's not dead. She's just sleeping."

Lump nudged me. "See. Maybe she's not dead after all."

But the mourners didn't see it that way. They started making fun of Jesus and saying stuff like "Ridiculous!" and "The craziest thing I ever heard."

"That's really rude!" Lump said. And he started shouting, "Stop that! Stop that!"

But I guess they thought they knew better. They were professional mourners, after all, and maybe they figured they knew a dead person when they saw one. So I tried to calm Lump down before they started laughing at him too. He didn't need that, on top of everything else.

It seemed like we waited for ages. And with all the wailing and crying, it was really hard. But I wasn't going to leave until Jesus came out that door again. And Lump and Bug felt just the same.

At last, the door began to open. I swallowed. Hard. Now I wasn't so sure I wanted to be there, to hear what had happened inside. Bug looked at the ground. And Lump crouched down and covered his face with his hands.

And then there he was, Rock Girl's dad.

"She's alive! Praise God! My daughter is alive!"

And he looked at the crowd. And he looked at the mourners. And he looked at me. I promise. And he shouted, "She's alive! Praise God! My daughter is alive!"

Everybody else started shouting too. And jumping up and down. Except for Lump, who was sobbing again. But good sobbing.

We pushed through to the front of the crowd.

"Can we see her?" Bug asked.

Rock Girl's dad smiled. "Sorry, boys. It's probably a bit too soon. She's just about to eat. She needs to get her strength back."

"It's hard to deny your daughter anything. Particularly when she's just come back from the dead."

"Are those my friends, Father?" called a familiar—and very alive—voice. "I'd love to talk to them. Please!"

Her dad sighed. "It's hard to deny your daughter anything. Particularly when she's just come back from the dead." Then he stepped out of the way. "Go on in. But make it quick."

We raced across the room to where Rock Girl was sitting. She grinned and opened her arms and went to stand up.

"No standing yet, dear," her mother said.

So we just stood there, smiling at her. And she smiled back. It was a little awkward at first. Talking with someone who had just been dead.

"So did you have that fever thing again?" Bug asked.

"I did," Rock Girl said. "And sweaty and shaky and pukey."

"And the other end?" Lump asked.

"And the other end." Rock Girl nodded, while her mom shook her head and sighed.

"Jesus told everybody you were asleep,"
I said.

"I did fall asleep," Rock Girl said. "And then
I guess I died. I don't know. I was asleep. Then I
heard somebody call for me, like you do when
your mom tries to wake you up. But it wasn't my
mom; it was Jesus. So I opened my eyes, and there
he was."

"What did he say?" Bug asked.

"He said my mom should make me something to eat."

"What are you going to have?" Lump asked.
"Cake? I think I would have asked for cake if I had
just come back from the dead."

"I think it's stew, actually," Rock Girl said.
"With meat and beans, I hope."

"Beans?" Lump said. "I hate beans! I think
I'd rather be dead than have to eat beans. Sorry."

"Well, I wouldn't!" Rock Girl said. "And I'm
glad I'm back!"

And then she looked at us like she was
expecting some kind of response. But the thing is,
you see, that she was still a girl, even if she wasn't
a girly girl, and so I didn't want it to sound like I
was glad she was back in a girl-boy kind of way.

And I don't think Bug wanted it to sound that way, either. But we *were* glad she was back, so it was, maybe for the first time, a good thing that Lump was there 'cause he can say anything to anybody and not have it come out in a girl-boy kind of way.

And that's what he did.

"Well, *we're* glad you're back," he said.

And Bug sort of mumbled a "Yeah," and I did too.

Then Lump walked over and gave her a big hug. And kind of giggled. And went all red.

And that more or less spoiled everything.

Chapter
Thirteen

WHERE LUMP TELLS A STORY THAT'S NOT ABOUT SOME GUY CALLED SAM

It was late. We had just finished eating. We were at Bug's uncle's house. And his aunt asked us the question that every kid hates to hear.

"So what did you boys do today?"

I don't know what adults expect. Do they

actually want a list? You know, an extended description from the moment we wake up and put on our clothes and eat our breakfast to whatever it is we do the rest of the day?

Or are they just being polite? Like when people ask you how you are and don't even pause for an answer?

Or maybe they just don't know what else to say. I dunno.

What I do know is that it can't possibly be because they'd find the answer interesting. Because most days, it's not.

I fed Penelope. I sold stuff. Not very gripping.

And that's why I said nothing.

And that's why Bug grunted something even I couldn't understand that sort of sounded like "Nothing."

"I heard a very interesting story today."

And that's why the conversation should have ended right there. Except that Lump was in the room.

"I heard a very interesting story today," he announced.

"It wasn't, by any chance, when you disappeared for most of the morning, was it?" Bug's dad grumbled.

"I don't think I ever really disappeared," Lump replied. "I'm pretty sure I was always visible. But it was in the morning, yes."

Now, you see, if Bug or I had answered that way, there would have been trouble. But Lump was so strange that even when he sounded like he was being a smart aleck, adults just chalked it up to his general weirdness. I was secretly sort of jealous. But I knew I could never be that bizarre, even if I tried.

"So what were you doing, then?" my dad asked.

"I was looking for ingredients for my models," Lump said (translation: collecting mud and straw and yes, a little poo), "when I saw Jesus talking with these men."

"What men?" Bug's aunt asked.

Lump looked at me. "Men like the ones we saw in the barley field," he said. "I think maybe your uncle Micah was there."

I glanced at Dad. He glanced back. We both rolled our eyes.

"Religious experts," Dad grunted. "Know-it-alls."

"It looked interesting," Lump went on. "So I went over and sat down on a wall, close enough to hear."

"Was it like an argument? A debate?" Sam asked. Just like Sam—always looking for a fight.

"Sort of." Lump hesitated. "It was like they were quizzing him."

"What kind of things did they ask?" I said.

Lump scratched his head. "Things like, why do camels only ask questions but never give answers?"

"Really?" Bug said. "Someone asked Jesus that?"

"No," Lump replied. "I think that came up in

my dream last night. It was a camel that asked it, as it happens. Which fits, if you think about it."

"We don't care about your dream!" Bug's dad broke in. "What did the men ask Jesus?"

"Something about living forever, I think," Lump answered. "That's it! How can we have eternal life?"

"So what did Jesus answer?" I said.

"He didn't!" Lump grinned. "He just asked a question back to the man. See, I knew there was something camelly going on."

"So what did Jesus ask?" Bug bugged.

"'What does our Law say?'" Lump remembered. "That's what he asked. And the man said that thing they say in the synagogue about loving God with your mind and soul and heart and strength. Oh, and loving your neighbor as yourself. Jesus told him it was a good answer."

"So no arguments, then?" Sam huffed.

Lump grinned again. "Not exactly. The man who asked the question started whispering to his friends. There was a lot of nodding and a little snickering too. Then the man turned around and asked Jesus another question: 'So who is my neighbor?'"

"And Jesus asked another question back, yeah?" I said, figuring Lump was just itching to mention that camel again.

"No," Lump said. "He did not. He told a story. A story about a man who walked from Jerusalem to Jericho."

Bug's dad shook his head. "Rough road, that. Thieves around every corner. I'd never take that road on my own."

Lump jumped. "That's what happened in the story. The man got robbed. They beat him and they took everything he had—even his clothes! And they left him for dead!"

Bug's aunt sucked in a big breath of air. "Ooh," she said. "Doesn't sound like a very nice story to me. That Jesus is supposed to be a holy man. But stories about violence and nakedness? I don't know . . ."

"It gets better!" Lump assured her. "I mean, in a less violent and naked way."

"Go on, then," she sighed. "I can always leave the room."

"In a little while, a priest came by," Lump said. "That's better, isn't it?"

"Much better." She smiled. "Good boy."

"So what do you think happened?" Lump asked.

"The priest prayed," my dad said.

"The priest helped the man," Bug's uncle said.

"The robbers were just hiding," Bug guessed, "so the priest ended up robbed and naked too!"

His aunt shot him a dirty look.

"The priest didn't do anything. He just went to the other side of the road and walked away."

But Lump could hardly contain himself. "Wrong, all wrong!" He beamed. "The priest didn't do anything. He just went to the other side of the road and walked away."

"Bit of an anticlimax, if you ask me," Bug's dad grunted.

My brother tapped his chin with his forefinger, in an annoying Uncle Micah way. "There could be a perfectly reasonable explanation for that," he said. "There was no way for the priest to know if the man was dead or not. If he had stopped to help and had touched him, and he was dead, then that would have made the priest unclean and he would not have been able to do his priestly duties."

"Or get his priestly pay, either," Bug's dad muttered. "A very 'reasonable' explanation."

"Violence. Nakedness. Nasty priests." Bug's aunt tut-tutted. "I thought you said this story got better."

"It does. It does." Lump nodded. "A man who worked in the Temple, an assistant to the priest, came by next. What do you think he did?"

Sam put a finger to his chin again. He was really starting to annoy me. "Well, if he wasn't that far behind the priest and saw the priest's very *reasonable* action, then I think he probably followed that example and crossed over to the other side of the road as well."

"That's . . . right," Lump said glumly. I knew he was hoping for some more wrong guesses.

"Is the man dead yet?" Bug asked. "You'd think he'd be dead by now."

And his aunt sighed.

"The man is not dead," Lump said.

"Thank goodness for that," Bug's aunt said.

"But he is still naked and beaten up and

could die at any time. So another man comes by. Somebody called Samaritan."

The room erupted in a chorus of disgust and disapproval.

"Samaritans?" Bug's dad grunted. "They're a bunch of half-breeds!"

"Heretics!" his uncle added.

"Traitors to our people," my dad said.

And quite surprisingly really, Bug's aunt spit on the floor.

"Not very popular, then?" I said. "Samaritans."

My brother. Finger. Chin. "According to Uncle Micah," he began (and I could have punched him. I really could have. But he punches back really hard, and there was already a lot of anger in the room), "when our people were taken away as captives by the Assyrians, those who were left behind married foreigners and worshiped their gods and built their own temple. They only accepted the books of Moses and rejected our prophets. And their land became a haven for criminals. Those are the Samaritans, and that is why we hate them."

Lump was laughing. Quietly. Like he was the only person in on the joke.

But Sam thought he was laughing at his explanation. "What's so funny, Weird Boy?" he grunted.

"Nothing." Lump chuckled. "Not you. No. It's just that it all makes sense now."

"What?" I asked.

"The story. See, I thought Jesus said the man's *name* was Sam. Sam Aritan, or something. I couldn't exactly hear. And I thought that maybe it was somebody he knew, and everybody else knew too. But what Sam—your brother, Sam—just said makes the story so much better!"

"So what did the Samaritan do?" Bug's aunt asked.

"Poked him with a stick, I bet," Bug's dad said.

"Hit him with a rock," Bug's uncle suggested.

"Finished him off for good!" said Bug, who obviously liked a good death scene.

"Just tell us," my dad sighed.

"He helped him," Lump replied. "The Samaritan! He helped the man who was beaten up and naked. He bandaged his cuts and put him on his donkey and took him to an inn. Then he gave the innkeeper lots of money to take care of the man and told him he would be back to see how he was doing. And that's why, when the story was finished, Jesus said the Samaritan was the man's neighbor."

The room was silent. Completely silent. And I think Lump took that as a good sign.

"Great story, isn't it?" He beamed.

But Lump was wrong. They weren't hanging on his every word. They were all just in shock.

"Stupidest thing I ever heard!" Bug's dad shouted. And he stormed out of the house.

"Complete waste of time!" moaned Bug's uncle, who stormed after him.

"Ridiculous. A fantasy," my brother sneered on his way out. "Totally detached from reality." And I so wanted to take that chin finger and stick it in his eye.

"I can't believe I'm saying this—" Bug's aunt rose to leave as well—"but I actually think I pre-ferred the nakedness and the violence."

"So did the man die while he was at the inn?" Bug asked.

I figured my dad would try to say something nice. At least I hoped so.

"Lump," he suggested, "sometimes it's best just to stick with what you know. Like those sculptures of yours. Amazing."

Well done, Dad, I thought. But Lump still looked really discouraged.

"I thought they'd like the story," he sighed. "Particularly once they heard that the person they thought was the villain turned out to be the good guy. It's like a surprise."

"Yeah, but not a good surprise," I said. "At least not where they're coming from."

"But that's what I like about Jesus," Lump said. "The surprises. Like when he healed my friend, even though he worked for a Roman. And when he asked that tax collector to be his disciple, even though he was a bully and a cheat. And when he said we should love our enemies and not fight with them. It's like he does the exact opposite of what you'd expect, of what people normally do. It's like he's not normal. Bit like me, maybe."

I didn't know what to say. I just sort of did my best.

"Yeah." I nodded. "You're both good at doing what's unexpected. That's for sure. And that's okay,

I guess, as long as you know that other people aren't always going to get it."

Then I had an idea.

"Listen," I said. "I could use some help feeding Penelope tonight. Want to come along? It's just normal stuff, but you can help, if you want."

Lump's eyes glowed, and he jumped up off the floor.

"I'd love to help!" he said.

So off we went. And even though I was pretty sure that there would still be some weirdness to come, I didn't mind. I felt pretty good, in fact. A bit like a Samaritan.

Chapter Fourteen

WHERE WE EAT BREAD AND FISH AND GO BROKE

"Where's Lump?" my dad asked.

"In Goofy Town," Sam sneered.

Now here's the thing. I know I have often said the same thing. And it's Weird Town, not Goofy Town. But Lump is my friend. Whereas Sam hardly recognizes his existence. Which is why I can say things like that, and why he cannot. Which is also why I said, "Shut your mouth!"

Which is also why he punched me.

Which is also why my dad sort of lost it.

"I have had enough of you two!" he shouted. "And your constant bickering. Can't you see that this is hard enough? Trying to make a living. Trying to find enough customers to keep going. And where is everybody, anyway?"

Fortunately Bug's dad showed up just in time to stop the rant.

"Everybody is on top of that hill!" he said, pointing. "Thousands and thousands of them."

"Why?" my dad asked.

"Jesus!" Bug's dad replied, slapping my dad on the back. "They're all up there listening to Jesus! Didn't I say this was a great idea?"

"But what good is that going to do us?" my dad said. "Our stalls are set up down here, in town."

Bug's dad grinned. "Which is where everyone will be coming when Jesus is finished talking. And what will they be when they get here? Hungry."

"They're hungry already!" Bug said.

"So hungry they could eat a . . . really big thing that would mean they weren't hungry anymore," Lump said.

"Ahhh, here they are," Bug's dad said. "The rest of our market research team, returned from the front lines."

"Goofy Town," my brother whispered. And I kicked him.

"There are stomachs grumbling everywhere up there," Bug said.

"So all we have to do is be ready to feed them when they come down," Bug's dad said.

"But we don't have food for thousands of people!" my dad replied.

"But we don't have food for thousands of people!"

"That's why we have to start buying it now!" Bug's dad said. "We take all the money we've got and we use it to buy something simple and cheap. I say lots of dried fish and bread. We position ourselves at the bottom of the hill, and as people come down, there we are! And we make a killing!"

My dad shook his head. "I don't know. All our money? It's a huge risk."

"It's a can't-miss golden opportunity," Bug's dad said. "That's what it is!"

So that's what we did. We took all our money and bought all the fish and bread we could find. And then Bug's dad had a second brilliant idea. He took a couple pieces of fish and five little loaves of bread and gave them to us.

"Take it up the hill, boys. Just walk around with it. Let the customers have a sniff. Then tell them where it came from!"

So Bug and Lump and I went up the hill with our fish and bread.

Jesus was still talking when we got there.

"Ooh," Lump said. "I heard Jesus say this bit before. It's good."

It was something about not worrying and trusting God to take care of you. I couldn't help thinking about what my dad had said in his little rant.

"Do you really think that works?" I said to Lump. "I mean, I trust my dad. But God? I'm not so sure."

Lump shrugged. "Dunno. But we've seen Jesus do some amazing things. So maybe he knows something we don't."

Just then, a man came running up to us.

"Boys," he said. "That fish, it smells wonderful."

"Thanks," Bug answered. And being his father's son, he took no time to add, "If you'd like some, you can buy it at the bottom of the hill!"

"Actually," the man replied, "what I'd like to do is . . . umm . . . borrow it."

"Borrow it?" I asked.

"Yeah . . . well . . . see, my name is Andrew," the man went on. "I'm one of Jesus' disciples, and he's looking for food to feed the crowd."

"So you're going to take the food to Jesus?" Bug said.

Andrew nodded.

"This is *perfect!*" Bug whispered to me. "If we can get Jesus to tell everybody how good this is, they'll all want some. And Dad will be really proud!"

He turned to Andrew. "Okay," he said, handing over the food. "You can take it to Jesus."

So Andrew took the food and we followed him to the place where Jesus was sitting with his other disciples.

"I found a boy, here, with five loaves and two fishes," Andrew said, pointing to Bug.

Jesus smiled and said, "Thank you."

Bug smiled back.

I did too.

But I thought Lump was going to pass out.

"I can't believe we're here! Right here! With him!" he whispered.

Then Jesus bowed his head and thanked God for the bread too.

And then, I don't know, I figured he'd probably take a bite or two, see if it was any good, maybe give a bit to his disciples, then tell the crowd where they could get some too.

But that's not what he did. Not by a long shot.

He broke the bread and the fish into pieces. And the more he broke, the more there was!

There's no way to really explain it. It's like there was a false bottom in the basket Bug gave him, with thousands of loaves and fishes hiding there. But there wasn't. And even that would have been impossible.

Loaf after loaf, fish after fish, it just kept coming!

It was one thing to see that paralyzed man walk or to see Rock Girl live again. Those miracles were amazing, yeah. But this was such an unexpected, bizarre, almost-crazy kind of thing, it was like . . . well, it was like Weird Town! But in the best possible way.

Bug and I just stood and stared.

And Lump really did end up fainting and only woke up when Andrew handed us some fish and bread too.

"Seems we have a lot of leftovers too."

"We really appreciate this," he said. "Thanks for your help. Oh, and feel free to take as much as you'd like with you. Seems we have a lot of leftovers too."

We sort of staggered back down the hill. Slowly. In a daze. Not only because of what had happened. But because of what was gonna happen.

"You know we're in a lot of trouble," Bug said.

"I do." I nodded.

"Why?" Lump asked. "People liked your fish. A lot!"

"They did," Bug agreed.

"And they are all really happy and full now," Lump said.

"They are," I said. "The only problem is that they are so full and so happy that none of them will be buying the fish and bread that our dads want to sell them on the way home."

And they didn't.

When we finally got to the stall, my dad and Bug's dad and Sam were doing their best to sell the food. But people kept burping and patting their stomachs and saying how they were already so full they couldn't possibly eat another bite.

"What happened?" Bug's dad asked us. "Did someone beat us to it? Was there food for sale up there?"

What could we say?

"Umm . . . well . . . you know," Bug mumbled. "Jesus . . . umm . . ."

"Yeah," I added. "Jesus. Amazing. What can we say?"

"I say we tell them the truth," Lump said. And now I thought I was going to faint.

"Jesus says we shouldn't worry and that we should trust God to take care of us," Lump

166 * Bob Hartman

said. "And up there, on the hill, he did. It was a miracle!"

I looked at my dad and Bug's dad and Sam and prayed that they wouldn't ask any more questions about that miracle. And they didn't.

"Well, it will be a miracle if we survive this can't-miss golden opportunity of yours," my dad said to Bug's dad. And he walked away, head hanging.

"Don't worry," Lump said.

"Don't be ridiculous, boy," Bug's dad said. "We're ruined. And it's all my fault." Then he walked off in the opposite direction.

"Goofy Town," Sam said, and he walked off too.

"Anybody want more fish?" Lump asked.

And Bug took a bit and chewed on it.

And I did too. And prayed for one more miracle.

WHERE WE FINISH UP WITH MORE QUESTIONS THAN ANSWERS

We had a lot of fish. We had a lot of bread.
And we had no money.

"I like fish and bread," Lump said. "But
maybe not enough to eat it for breakfast. And
lunch. And dinner. For a month."

"Don't think you have to worry about that," Bug sighed. "It'll all be rotten or moldy in a couple of days."

"Which is why we have to sell it now!" Bug's dad said.

Which would have been a great idea if everyone in town hadn't been climbing into boats and setting off across the sea.

"Where are they going?" I asked.

My dad sighed. "Well, rumor has it that your buddy Jesus crossed the sea, in the night. And everyone figures if they cross the sea, too, and catch up with him, that he'll feed them again."

"Which is another perfect opportunity for us!" Bug's dad said. "We have all the fish in town. And his stock has to run out eventually."

"What do we have to lose?"

I looked at Bug. Bug looked at me. And Lump grinned and whispered, "I wouldn't be so sure."

"I say we get in a boat and follow the crowd," Bug's dad suggested. "What do we have to lose?"

I looked at Sam and snickered, "Our lunch?"

And he punched me.

"Not much," my dad said, "seeing as we've already pretty much lost everything. But how are we going to pay for the ride?"

Fortunately, or unfortunately, the only boat left to hire belonged to our crazy captain friend (no surprise there). And he was happy to sail us across in exchange for some of our fish and bread. And one of Lump's models. A whale, with a little Jonah hanging out of its mouth.

"It be a fine day fer sailing," he said. "Aaar!"

And it was. The sky was blue. The sea was too. And Sam was only a tiny bit green.

When we got to the other side, there was

Jesus and the crowd. But no sign of either fish or bread.

Bug's dad slapped my dad on the back. "I think we made the right decision this time," he said.

And I think I heard my dad mutter something like "For once."

I say, "I think" because just as we climbed out of the boat, Andrew, the guy we met the day before, came rushing up to us.

"Don't give him any food! Whatever he says!" Bug whispered.

But he didn't ask for food.

"Just wanted to say hi," Andrew said. "Was your trip okay?"

"Very pleasant," Lump said. "And yours?"

Andrew laughed. "Pretty much the opposite of pleasant. We left last evening, and when we were about three or four miles out, we ran into a storm."

"So Jesus stood up in the boat," Lump said, "and made the storm calm down?"

"Nooo," Andrew said, giving Lump a *how did you know that?* look. "Jesus actually wasn't in the boat."

"Where was he, then?" Bug asked.

Andrew bent down and whispered, "You're not going to believe this."

Bug whispered back, "After yesterday, I bet we will."

"He was walking on the water," Andrew said.

And all three of us said, "No way!"

"You're not going to believe this."

"You could not make this stuff up," Andrew said. "We were pretty scared, anyway, what with the storm and all, but when somebody saw a figure out on the sea, we were terrified."

"I bet you thought it was a ghost!" Lump said.

"We did!" Andrew replied.

"I love ghosts!" Lump said.

"But then he spoke," Andrew said, "and we knew it was Jesus."

"I bet you were disappointed," Lump said. "Because it wasn't a ghost."

"No, no," Andrew said. "We were confused because we'd left him up on the mountain praying and didn't expect him to be there. And we were shocked and surprised, naturally."

"Because he hadn't told you he was coming?" Lump said.

Andrew looked at me and Bug, puzzled. "No, because he was, you know, walking. On the water."

"So what happened next?" I asked.

Andrew sighed. "My brother decided to do something kind of stupid."

"Tell me about it," I said. "Brothers are the worst."

"The thing is," Andrew said, "my brother Peter doesn't always think before he acts. So before any of us could stop him, he asked Jesus if he could walk on the water *with* him."

"And what did Jesus say?" Bug asked.

"Come on in—er . . . out, I guess!" Andrew said. "So Peter did. And honestly, for a tiny little while, he was walking on the water too! But then I think he realized what he'd gotten himself into and got scared. I mean, who wouldn't? He started to sink, so Jesus grabbed hold of him and helped him back into the boat."

"And the storm?" Lump asked.

Andrew nodded. "And that's when the storm stopped. And that's when we . . . well . . . worshiped him."

"What, like he was God?" I said.

"I guess. He's a really hard guy to pin down," Andrew said. "He's something special, that's for sure. Not just a teacher. Not just a healer. You saw it yourself. He fed all those people with your lunch. He stills storms. He walks on water. Who else could he be?"

"He fed all those people with your lunch. He stills storms. He walks on water. Who else could he be?"

Just then, a lot of booing erupted from the

crowd. And a lot of people started to climb back into their boats.

Bug's dad ran over to us.

"Hurry, boys," he said. "I think our moment has finally arrived!"

"What happened?" Bug asked.

And his dad laughed. "Seems like Jesus ran out of fish."

"Impossible!" Lump shouted.

"Well, at the very least," Bug's dad said, "he told everybody that they weren't getting anything else to eat and that they should stop following him if they were only doing it for a free lunch. Then he went on and on about how *he* was the bread they needed. And I pretty well got lost at that point."

"So the people are going to buy their lunch from us?" Bug asked.

His dad pointed to the stall, which was buzzing. "Looks like it!" he said.

"We'd better get going," I said to Andrew.

"Sounds like I need to do the same thing," he said. "You never can tell what Jesus will do next. See you around."

So Bug and Lump and I joined the others at the stall. And yes, it was the miracle I had prayed

for. We made back all the
money we had lost and a lot
more. And everybody was
happy, I guess.

But I couldn't stop
thinking about Jesus.

Who was he? Really?

I watched Andrew and the other disciples
walk away with him. Was he the Son of God?

I saw those three ladies, the ones who said
they gave him money to support him. Was Jesus
the Messiah, like they thought?

I looked at Lump, who loved the things he
taught. Was Jesus simply a great rabbi?

I looked at Bug and his dad. Was he nothing
more than a golden opportunity?

Then I looked at my own dad, and yeah, at
my brother. And I thought about my mom. And I
couldn't help but wonder. Was Jesus someone who
helped other people, but who had come along too
late to help us?

I didn't know. And I guess I figured that the
only way to find out was to keep on following him.

About
the
Author

Bob Hartman is a pastor, author, and
storyteller with a rich history in publishing and
whose books have sold more than one million copies. Primarily, he's written Bible storybooks and
children's books with strong moral themes. Bob
is best known for *The Lion Storyteller Bible*, which
has sold more than 200,000 copies, and *The Wolf
Who Cried Boy*, with more than 90,000 copies sold.
He is also the author of YouVersion's Bible App for
Kids, which has been downloaded over five million
times. Bob is married to Sue, and they have two
married children and three grandchildren.